The Appraisal 2

The Appraisal 2

Brielle Montgomery

www.urbanbooks.net

Urban Books, LLC
300 Farmingdale Road, NY-Route 109
Farmingdale, NY 11735

The Appraisal 2

ISBN 13: 978-1-64556-453-9
ISBN 10: 1-64556-453-3

First Mass Market Printing March 2023
First Trade Paperback Printing March 2022
Printed in the United States of America

10 9 8 7 6 5 4 3 2 1

Distributed by Kensington Publishing Corp.
Submit Orders to:
Customer Service
400 Hahn Road
Westminster, MD 21157-4627
Phone: 1-800-733-3000
Fax: 1-800-659-2436

The Appraisal 2

by

Brielle Montgomery

Diary Entry 34:

I don't play fair. Revenge is not meant to be. Strategy Part 1: Divide. Bitch has underestimated me. . . .

CHAPTER ONE

Jayla

The obituary initially brought on a sense of déjà vu.

Jayla remembered feeling this same nostalgia nearly twelve years before at her mother's funeral. She remembered standing at the cemetery, between her sisters, guilty tears dampening her cheeks as she eyed the glistening cherrywood casket, its entire length adorned with an array of rich purple and pink lilies. She remembered the sun being excruciatingly hot as it beamed down on her all-black dress. And her poor sister, Jackie's voice hitching and wavering throughout the entire eulogy as she sobbed repeatedly. It was an emotional service, but Jayla remembered that part of her, a small part, was still bitter about what her mother had done to her. Because of that, she didn't allow herself to feel sadness. But that still didn't stop the guilt that clawed at the pit of her stomach as she stood amid the family who loved her mother dearly, knowing the truth behind her death.

Jayla shook her head now at the memory. She swallowed hard as she stared at the woman's face on the paper, a mixture of anger and sadness causing tears to sting the corners of her eyes. She should have been able to attend this funeral. Even if it had been under such strict conditions. Of course, she wouldn't have been able to mingle with her family or ride in the family car during the procession. She would have been handcuffed and chaperoned by two armed deputies, who would have watched her like a hawk. The whole scene would have been embarrassing. But, dammit, she had been looking forward to that day ever since she'd assumed the warden would sign her authorization to attend the funeral. Never had she expected Aunt Beverly's death, but to be honest, she had been so damn busy enjoying the prospect of being outside the jail walls after fourteen months that she really hadn't given much thought to grieving.

Her brother-in-law and on-again, off-again lover, Quentin, had sent a letter to accompany the obituary, and Jayla found comfort in the thoughtful gesture. He had been the only one to write her about Aunt Bev. Her sister Jackie had not been considerate enough to inform her of their aunt's passing. She would harp on that later. For now, she needed to see a certain prison guard. That bitch had some serious explaining to do.

Jayla threw her feet over the side of the top bunk and hopped down off the hard mattress. Confinement had turned her once glowing skin ashen brown and had sharpened her soft features. Gone was the luxury of a gorgeous mane of hair bouncing at her shoulders. Jayla's natural tresses and high ponytail had become just as much a part of her as the hideous jail uniform.

After heading through her open cell doorway, Jayla made her way past the row of eight-by-five cells overlooking a general common area. The low hum of the TV echoed from the recreation room, but after six consecutive days of rain, the little piece of sun in the yard had most of the inmates opting to go outside today. She nodded toward a cluster of inmates posted on the stairs leading to the residential wing and quickened her pace.

Even though she had shed a few pounds, Jayla still had her signature curves, and the dingy sweat-pants and oversize county jail T-shirt did little to hide them. The women wanted her sexy ass, she knew, but none of them would dare fuck with her. Not with Dreena being her cellmate. Not to mention that her and Correctional Officer Banks's little arrangement kept them at bay. They didn't want that problem. So, she trotted down the steps, almost feeling the air dampen with the cream from their kitties.

A prison guard was on post by a wall in the common area and was standing stoically against a stack of foldable chairs. Jayla eyed the face and remembered this guard was one of the newer ones on this shift.

"Hey," she said, stopping in front of the woman. "I'm looking for Officer Banks."

The woman narrowed her eyes at Jayla. "What for?"

Jayla pursed her lips to keep from snapping. These new folks always thought they ran some shit. "Because she requested to see me," she lied.

It was obvious the guard didn't believe her, but this woman, too, knew Officer Banks was the head bitch in charge. The guard frowned, conflicted about the idea of giving in to an inmate but concerned about feeling the wrath of her boss if the request was true and she ignored it.

"Fine," she sighed, relenting. "Wait here." She pulled her walkie-talkie from her belt and clicked the side button twice to send an alert.

A voice came through the static. “Go ahead, Officer Kline.”

“Yes, Officer Banks, you are needed in the general common area.”

A pause. “Roger that.”

A few moments later, an overweight woman with a matted red wig and lips black from too many cigarettes pushed through the secure door that led to a set of offices. Jayla stifled a grimace as the woman’s lips curled into a familiar smile, showing a set of dingy yellow teeth.

“Inmate Morgan.” Her voice was raspy as she greeted Jayla by the customary last name. She nodded toward the hall. “Come with me.”

Obediently, Jayla followed her down the hall, and after she entered Banks’s closet-sized office, she waited as Banks closed the door behind her.

“What’s up, girl?” Banks said casually as she waddled around her cluttered desk and took a seat. “What do you need?”

Jayla bit her tongue, struggling to restrain her anger. “You said I would get approved to go to my aunt’s funeral. What happened?”

Banks sat back in the seat, and it groaned loudly under her unbearable weight. “I told you I would try,” she said with a nonchalant shrug. “I’m sorry. I tried. Your aunt is not considered immediate family, so—”

"Fuck that!" Jayla snapped, itching to throw something at the guard's smug face. "You told me I would be able to go. Damn, Banks. That's fucked up."

Banks was unfazed by the outburst. She pulled open the top drawer of her desk and snatched a piece of candy from the pile. "I tried," she repeated as she unwrapped the chocolate and shoved it into her mouth. "Like I said, I'm not the warden. Only he approves these authorizations, and he said no dice. What the hell did you expect me to do? Break you outa here myself?"

Jayla gave in to the temptation to swipe her arm across the stacks of papers littering the desk, sending them flying across the room. She was seething. "Bitch, you made me eat your pussy because you guaranteed you would get me an approval. I trusted you." Just the thought of how her head had been buried between the officer's fat thighs, how she'd lapped the folds of her rank-ass pussy brought on a wave of nausea. But she had thought it would be worth it.

For some reason, Banks found the tantrum hilarious, and she howled in laughter, exposing the melted chocolate on her tongue and teeth. "Oh, it didn't feel like you minded that," she said. "Just a minor inconvenience. But like I said, what the hell do you want me to do? Shit, she's buried now."

Jayla clenched her fists, but she knew she wouldn't dare punch this woman in her face. Banks didn't care if they had been looking out for one another before. She probably wouldn't hesitate to put Jayla's ass in isolation if she stepped too far outside her "prisoner" boundaries. Frustrated, Jayla turned and stormed toward the door. She needed some fucking air.

"I don't see what the big deal is, girl," Banks called after her. "You ain't got but four more months left."

Jayla walked out, slammed the door behind her, and groaned. She had never before experienced this kind of backstabbing with Banks. The officer had always looked out for her. Had always helped her out. Had kept the other inmates from gang-raping her ass since day one. She had slid Jayla everything from snacks to liquor and anything else she needed. In exchange, Jayla didn't mind fucking her from time to time. She had long since ignored her HIV results and had put herself to work doing what she did best. It was the only way she was going to survive.

She could kill Jasmine, her backstabbing bitch of a daughter, for putting her in this position. It was bad enough the bitch was out of control, but as the days passed, Jayla's anger and thirst for revenge could only marinate. She hadn't been too worried about the solicitation for prostitution charges that Heather, the arresting officer, had threatened her with. She'd figured those misdemeanors were hard to prove and wouldn't hold up in court. But then they had started talking about pimping and pandering, because Jayla had gotten Jasmine involved in the appraisal business. The operation was simple: women paid Jayla to determine their men's worth by "appraising" them. In other words, she was paid to tempt them to see if they would cheat. So what if it was exploitation? Men eventually cheated. They always did.

Knowing that bitch, Jasmine had already been singing like a fucking canary, and Jayla hadn't wanted to suffer the consequences. Then the police had started spitting out more serious terms, like felony and maximum-security prison. So Jayla had jumped on the DA's plea deal, though she'd dreaded having to serve the eighteen-month sentence in state jail. But she'd been putting the time behind bars to good use by dedicating each day to plotting how she was going to destroy Jasmine.

After leaving Banks's office, Jayla went out into the courtyard. The sun did little to lessen the chill of the crisp October air. Women prisoners were perched on the multiple picnic tables spread across the dead lawn. Everyone wore the same sweatpants and T-shirts with the words STATE PRISONER printed across the back like a warning sign. Off to one side, a basketball game was in full swing, and prison guards stood at posts along the mesh razor wire lining the courtyard.

As she gazed around, Jayla noticed her cellmate, Dreena, shooting dice among a group of women. The woman was a pure butch, from her burly frame, which bulged in her worn-out uniform, to her cornrow braids, which she always managed to talk some scared chick into keeping fresh for her. She was usually either in isolation or on her way back to isolation. It was only a matter of time before her firecracker temper had her slamming some helpless woman's face into a cinder-block wall.

A few women nodded in Jayla's direction as she made her way to a patch of dead grass and sat down Indian-style. She found peace in this little spot because not only could she watch all the activity in the courtyard, but she could also look out through the fence, silently aching for the freedom that lay beyond the parking lot.

Jayla still clutched Quentin's letter in her fist. She finally uncrumpled the loose-leaf paper and scanned the neatly written handwriting. She smiled as certain sentences jumped off the page. *I miss you. Can't wait to see you again.* It was obvious he had remembered when they were together all those years ago, despite the fact that he was her sister's husband.

In his last letter he'd said he had left her sister. Jayla hadn't asked why. She hadn't really given a damn, to be honest. She didn't care if he actually meant anything he wrote in these letters, but she did relish the attention he gave her. And the hope. It kept her sane. Besides, she was slightly happy that Jackie was gone, even in only for the moment. It meant that Quentin still didn't know that Jayla had tried to turn their daughter out in the heart appraisal game. Not that her actions had been malicious. In fact, Jasmine had wanted in, and Jayla had trusted she could handle the responsibility. But that didn't make it look any better, and her ass was as good as dead if Quentin ever found out. And other than Patricia, her hands-on mentor and lover, and the woman who had got her involved in the business, Quentin was all Jayla had.

"Jayla."

Jayla glanced up and squinted through the piercing sun. The sight of the woman's silhouette had her on her feet in an instant. Mona was usually quiet, but Jayla remembered the bitch had tried her only a month into her sentence. Even though she was so skinny, she had enormous strength, and the ass whupping she had put on Jayla over some damn juice in the commissary had Jayla on guard. Granted, Mona hadn't fucked with her since then, but Banks wasn't around right now and Dreena was still across the yard.

"What's up?" Mona asked. She tilted her head and stared Jayla down as she ran her hand across the short spikes of her pixie cut.

Jayla frowned, refusing to speak until she could assess the situation.

"Look, I ain't trying to start no shit with you," Mona assured her, lifting her hands in mock surrender. "This is business."

Jayla relaxed a little. She knew exactly what *business* Mona was talking about, but the woman had never struck her as the type to be into that type of thing. "What you got?" she asked.

"I got some chips from the commissary." Mona lowered her voice when she added, "Barbecue."

"Bitch, really?" Jayla frowned. "Some fucking chips from the commissary? Please. You ain't seeing shit with that weak-ass exchange."

Mona glanced around, clearly uneasy about the conversation. "Okay, okay," she said, relenting. "My sister was able to sneak in some Grey Goose. I got a few ounces in the cell."

"How many?"

"Three."

Jayla narrowed her eyes, not sure if the woman was lying or not. "I want it all," she said firmly. "And don't bullshit me. I'll come pick it up after dinner, and if you try some shit, I'm sure Dreena wouldn't mind waxing that kitty of yours. You got it?"

Mona nodded and shuffled off.

Jayla grinned. She had really come up off her little prison hustle. She never would've thought it would be so profitable, but these horny bitches were bartering out the ass for a glimpse of the action. It was amusing.

When the guards began their routine shift change, Jayla sprinted toward the door. The rotation meant rec was about over and the guards would soon be rounding up the inmates for dinner. Which meant she had a good ten minutes to use the phone before the others would be fighting over it.

As soon as she got to the phone, Jayla punched in the familiar number, and after she listened to the monotone operator, she heard Patricia's voice come through the phone like a refreshing burst of air.

"Puma, I was waiting for your call," she said, using her pet name for Jayla. "Damn, I miss you."

"I miss you too. Not too much longer."

"I'm glad you called." Patricia lowered her voice, as if someone had just walked in the room, and added, "I've got an opportunity for you when you come home. You know, to get you back on your feet."

She had definitely managed to pique Jayla's interest. The hint was subtle, but Patricia's voice told her this was something other than a simple referral for a regular nine-to-five. "Well, you know I'm retired," Jayla replied. Every word was being recorded, so she definitely didn't want to incriminate herself.

"I know," Patricia said. "But trust me, Puma. This is something you need to hear. I promise you. I'll be down there day after tomorrow so we can chat."

Genuine excitement had Jayla grinning. It always felt good to have Patricia visit. Hell, anyone, for that matter, but Patricia had been the only one ever to make the trip. "I can't wait."

"Me either, Puma. Stay strong. It's almost over."

Jayla sighed. Having her freedom and her life ripped right out from under her was something she had never been able to come to terms with. Yes, she had managed to tolerate life in prison the best she could, but a piece of her died inside with each laborious day behind bars. “I love you,” she whispered into the receiver.

“I love you too,” Patricia replied, then ended the call.

Jayla sat the phone back on the hook, and her thoughts wandered to Patricia’s “opportunity.” Her mind spun with possibilities, but she couldn’t imagine any scenario that was so ideal that Patricia could wait to discuss it in person.

The doors banged open, and she heard the first few inmates spill into the jail, their voices a blur. As they all shuffled to their scheduled destination, Jayla turned and headed down the hall to blend in with the masses. Whatever Patricia had to say would have to wait for now. She had to have dinner, and then she had to get ready for business tonight. It was going to be a little different than usual, and she could not wait.

Jayla watched the hands on the clock tick away, and pretty soon, they were all being dismissed from dinner. Her tin tray still contained a skimpy portion of beef stew, which always tasted like the aluminum can the cooks had dumped it out of. Thankfully, quite a few inmates paid her in food that their visiting family members had brought or that they had snuck from the guards’ cafeteria, so she knew she would be munching on some ribs and red velvet cake later. She just had to wait until 9:00 p.m. Then she would be open for business.

Jayla dumped her tray and stacked her chair against the wall. She then crossed into the day room and plopped down on the grungy sofa. Someone had the mounted TV on some talk show, but Jayla ignored the boring discussion on the screen. She scanned the crowd, searching for Dreena. When she didn't see her, she figured Dreena was already making her rounds to pick up the "fee" from the inmates who were going to participate tonight. One thing was for sure, Dreena was loyal.

Finally, the burly woman in question strolled into the day room, a cigarette bobbing in the corner of her mouth, her eyes squinting through the haze. Her gaze landed on Jayla, and she smiled as she made her way over to the sofa.

"Did Mona have liquor?" Jayla asked as soon as Dreena had taken a seat next to her.

"Hell yeah. About ten ounces. Bitch has been holding out."

Lying bitch. Jayla frowned at the thought as Dreena pulled the cigarette from her lips and passed it over. Grateful, Jayla took a long drag from the stick and noted that the nicotine was laced with weed. As if on cue, her tense muscles began to relax one by one. Leave it to Dreena. "I hope you cleaned her ass out," Jayla sighed, then puffed once more and blew a stream of smoke into the air.

"Damn sure did." Dreena reached into her breast pocket and pulled out a rusty flask. She twisted off the cap and held it out for Jayla. "Might as well get a pre-buzz," she said.

Jayla accepted the flask and knocked back the liquor, letting the liquid sting the back of her throat. She took a few more swallows before she passed back the flask.

When the clock hit 8:42 p.m., inmates started wrapping it up and trickling from the day room. Jayla nodded at Dreena, and they both rose from the sofa. Jayla followed right behind Dreena as they made their way back to the cells.

Sure enough, JC, an overweight dyke who was always the prison favorite, sat waiting on the top bunk in her cell. She was completely naked. Other prisoners had made themselves comfortable in her cell. Jayla slid in and off to one side to get a premium view, while Dreena continued down the hall.

At five minutes to nine, Dreena appeared at the barred door to JC's cell, her hand wrapped around Mona's bound wrists. Mona was completely naked, with the exception of the sock that had been stuffed in her mouth and the clear tape across her cheeks, which kept the gag in place. She looked as if she had been crying. Jayla turned away after glimpsing the shock in the woman's eyes.

A few months into Jayla's sentence, about the time that Dreena had started her stint on the line, the two had come up with a great way to ease their challenges in jail. Sex. And to think women were willing to pay to watch. It was a niche and an untapped "revenue" stream, and with Banks providing her the necessary security coverage, Jayla was able to organize underground live porn with no problems. She was hoping tonight wouldn't be any different.

She really had not intended for this afternoon to be a coincidence. Mona had just approached her in the courtyard, wanting to watch the scheduled sexcapade between JC and whichever woman was willing to partake. But a few weeks before, Jayla had suggested to Dreena that Mona should be their next leading lady. When Dreena had responded that she probably wouldn't be willing, Jayla had merely chuckled. "Who said Mona needs to be willing?" she had responded with a smirk. "This shit is business. She doesn't have a choice."

Dreena pushed a crying Mona into the crowded cell, and she stumbled and fell to her knees. Her body quivered, and her pleas for help bounced off the cell walls. JC's eyes were filled with a lustful thirst as she jumped down from the bunk. Jayla watched along with the other women as JC pulled Mona's face to her chest and began caressing her hair. She then laid the woman back and kissed her inner thigh. Mona started squirming from either fear or ecstasy. Jayla couldn't be sure which, but it really didn't matter. This would be the first instance where both parties were not consenting, but Mona's tears and the restraints only heightened the sexual tension in the cell.

JC had just pried open Mona's slender legs, and now she began making her way to Mona's hairy pussy. She planted a gentle kiss on the woman's clit before she began licking feverishly, much to the pleasure of every woman watching. Mona moaned, and she looked as if she was struggling to fix her lips to say, "Stop!" as JC feasted.

"What the fuck is going on here?" Banks's voice lifted above the noise of the crowd. Everyone froze. Even JC lifted her head, her lips glistening with Mona's juices.

Jayla frowned at Dreena as Banks stepped into the cell with two prison guards in tow. The bitch was acting brand new. She knew damn well what was going on.

Banks scanned the crowd and smiled when her beady eyes landed on Jayla. "Bingo," she said and pointed in her direction. "Grab that one." She gestured toward Dreena. "And that one. And lock their asses in solitary."

Jayla didn't even fight back as the guard grabbed her arm and snatched her toward the door of the cell. She kept her gaze fixed on Banks, a mixture of shock and anger narrowing her eyes to dangerous slits. The bitch had double-crossed her again.

As if on cue, Banks said, "Looks like you won't be getting out in a few months like you thought. Next time, you watch who you run your mouth to. I think you forgot that I'm the head bitch in charge around here. Not you."

Before Jayla could snap back with a response, she was pulled from the cell and hauled down the stairs toward the solitary confinement wing. She heard Dreena behind her cussing and resisting. But she figured she needed to cooperate. She was praying damn hard that this little sting operation wouldn't fuck up her sentence. But the thing was that Jayla didn't know what that bitch Banks had the power to do. And for that reason alone, Jayla was scared.

CHAPTER TWO

Jasmine

Something was very wrong.

Jasmine shifted uncomfortably on the exam table and averted her eyes from the blank ultrasound machine. He didn't know about the pregnancy, but Jasmine couldn't help but wonder why the sex had been so rough last night. Rougher than usual. Of course, she had ignored the cramps clenching her abdominal muscles with every painful thrust, but she damn sure hadn't expected the quarter-size droplets of blood that stained her underwear this morning.

Jasmine rubbed her belly in an effort to feel the familiar nudge against her palm. She had gotten used to her baby's morning workout, so the fact that her stomach remained still had induced the fear piercing through her body. *If I lose the baby . . .* Jasmine shook her head to dispel the dreaded thought. She couldn't afford to think that way. She needed this baby. Her life damn near depended on it.

"Knock, knock." Dr. Molina cracked open the door and poked her head through. Her kind eyes focused on her patient through the lenses of her black-framed glasses. She smiled, a weak attempt to ease the discomfort in the room. "How are you feeling?"

Jasmine sighed and struggled to steady her breathing. "I would be better if I knew what was going on," she admitted.

She watched the young Hispanic woman make her way across the room. Her heart slammed against her chest in such quick succession, her heartbeat felt more like a steady vibration. Even more so when she watched the doctor's forehead crease from apparent concern as she studied the clipboard in her hands. "What is it?" Jasmine's voice was nearly a whisper.

"No worries," Dr. Molina said as she laid the clipboard on the nearby table. That practiced smile of hers was planted on her face once again. "I can definitely understand your concern, but I'm sure there is nothing to worry about. Let's just have a look here."

Jasmine closed her eyes and let out a staggered breath. She wasn't a praying woman, but she found herself mouthing a plea to God anyway. Just in case.

Dr. Molina hummed some offbeat tune as she positioned herself on the stool between Jasmine's legs. "No hubby this time?" she said.

"No," Jasmine answered dismissively. She frowned when Dr. Molina didn't take the hint.

"I was sure he would accompany you this time," she went on, snapping on latex gloves as she spoke. "I would've loved to meet him."

"Maybe next time," Jasmine mumbled. This was the same lie she repeated at each appointment. Each and every visit, the ob-gyn staff questioned her in a subtle way about her solo trips to their office. Jasmine was sure they found it strange that she always came alone, despite being seven months along now.

Jasmine closed her eyes as she felt the cool gel being smeared on her belly. She held her breath, and when she felt the gentle pressure of the transducer, she risked a fearful peek at the monitor.

As expected, the image of her baby crystalized, concentrated shades of gray and black coming in and out of focus, as Dr. Molina moved the wand over her abdomen. The silence hung thick as excruciating seconds ticked by.

Where is the heartbeat? Why isn't the baby moving? Jasmine wondered.

When Dr. Molina frowned at the screen, Jasmine felt the fear clutch her throat and take what little bit of breath she had left. She struggled to lift herself up onto her elbows to get a closer look. "What?"

"Just wait a minute." Dr. Molina's voice carried a practiced reassurance but did little to ease Jasmine's rising panic. She continued to massage Jasmine's tummy with the wand, attempting to coax some sort of reaction from the motionless fetus. Nothing.

Jasmine's heart tightened and throbbed against her chest like a fist hitting her rapidly. She began trembling with such vigor that she felt like she would shake herself right off the exam table. *Not again*, she thought and shut her eyes against the piercing reality as the silence continued to suffocate her. *Not again. Not again. Not—*

The sudden whooshing sound of the baby's heartbeat had Jasmine snapping her head to the monitor. Sure enough, the collection of tissue silhouetting the baby's tiny frame began to bend and stretch. The tiny heartbeat echoed through the tiny room. Jasmine grinned as she let out a grateful sigh.

"Oh, you gave us a little scare, darling," Dr. Molina cooed at the screen. "Did we wake you up?"

Jasmine stifled the urge to leap off the table and hit a cartwheel. "She's really okay?" she asked, just to make sure.

Dr. Molina laid the wand down and sighed. "Yes," she answered. "But I need you to take it easy.

This is a very delicate time, and given your prior miscarriages—"

"Should I be concerned?"

"I'm going to recommend bed rest," Dr. Molina said. "Just as a safety precaution."

Jasmine frowned. There was no way in hell she could spend the next two months confined to a bed. "I can't do that," she murmured.

Now it was Dr. Molina's turn to frown. "Can't or won't?" When Jasmine remained silent, she continued. "Listen, I can't tell you what to do. But as your doctor, I'm trying to look out for the health and safety of both you and baby. We've already had a few complications, so I suggest just staying off your feet as much as possible. No lifting whatsoever. No laundry, no groceries . . . Get hubby to handle that for you." She used a tissue to wipe the gel from Jasmine's stomach. "Take this time to enjoy being able to relax, because Lord knows, when baby gets here, you'll wish you had." She laughed at the simple joke, and Jasmine merely nodded.

Precaution or not, that bed-rest shit wasn't going to fly.

After Dr. Molina left the exam room, Jasmine stood to get dressed, flicking her fourteen-inch Brazilian weave ponytail over her shoulder. Her stomach had certainly expanded during her pregnancy, but she was proud that her face had not ballooned too. She had definitely thickened, so she filled the hell out of her clothes, but Jasmine refused to step out in anything less than her Michael Kors heels and size eight skinny leg jeans. Her baby wasn't everybody's business, so Jasmine concealed her protruding belly by wearing ruffled shirts and cardigans. Only a few more months to go and her plan would fall easily into place. In the meantime, she needed some lunch.

Her bright mood immediately dissipated when she left the ob-gyn office. As she approached her pearl-white Bentley in the parking lot, she saw a familiar woman perched comfortably on top of it. Jasmine's lips creased into a frown, and she rolled her eyes, not bothering to hide the gesture of irritation.

The woman waited patiently, seemingly unbothered by the scowl planted on Jasmine's face. She was entirely overdressed for a casual summer Saturday, sporting a yellow silk blouse without sleeves that hung over the waist of her white designer pants. Her hair had grown long enough to flutter around her ears, and the brown tint easily hid her gray strands.

"The hell are you doing here?" Jasmine snapped. "And get your ass off of my car."

"Well, hello to you too." The woman smiled, removing the large-lensed shades adorning her face. "I've been trying to call you."

Jasmine sucked her teeth. "Obviously, I don't want to talk to you. You act like you don't have a fucking clue."

"Why won't you answer my calls?"

"The better question is, why the hell are you bothering me, Patricia?"

Patricia smiled warmly, almost motherly. "You know your mother wants me to look out for you."

Her gentle smile only heightened Jasmine's anger. "Please. That is not my fucking mother." She suddenly felt her baby kick, and she took a labored breath, struggling to calm down. "I wish you would stop saying that," she went on. Her tone was a little softer now but was laced with just as much tension. "Jayla is not my mother."

"She wants me to keep an eye on you—"

"An eye on me?" Jasmine's head whipped around at the absurdity of the statement. "Patricia, what you and that bitch need to realize is that I'm grown. I don't need anybody to keep an eye on me. You see that car you're sitting on?" Jasmine gestured to the Bentley and watched Patricia spare the car a sideways glance. "Yeah. That's my shit. I've got money, and I've got a man who loves me, so clearly, I must be doing something right."

Patricia turned up her nose and eyed the car once more. "Yeah, I'll bet you're doing something right."

"Really, Patricia?" Jasmine narrowed her eyes at the subtle innuendo. "You, of all people, are going to judge me? The fuck does it matter to you? I'm well taken care of. Trust."

"Look, I'm not trying to argue." Patricia's sigh was heavy with agitation. "She's worried about you. I'm worried about you. You are trying to disappear, but you can't run from the truth."

The baby kicked again, this time with enough force to send a wave of pain rippling through Jasmine's spine, and she felt her legs giving out a little. She keeled over and bared her teeth against the piercing pain as Patricia rushed to her side.

"Jasmine, what—"

"I'm fine." She threw up her arm to ward off the woman's assistance. "Just leave me alone. You're stressing me out. Damn." Jasmine winced as she gathered herself and rose to her feet. Then she stumbled toward her car. She hoped like hell Patricia couldn't tell she was pregnant.

"Jasmine, can we just go somewhere and talk? I have something to tell you."

The statement had Jasmine pausing at her car door. She cast a doubtful look over her shoulder. "What is it?"

Patricia glanced around, as if she was making sure no one was within earshot. "It's private," she said. "But it's important. Five minutes. Can you just give me five minutes?"

Jasmine rolled her eyes and snatched open her car door. *Just another tactic*, she thought. Patricia and Jayla were so much alike, it was damn near nauseating. She could almost bet the woman didn't have shit worthy to say.

"Stay the hell away from me, Patricia," she mumbled, sliding onto the crisp leather driver's seat of her car. "You keep harassing me, shit is going to get real ugly, real fast. You got that?" She slammed the door shut and was slightly surprised when Patricia made no move to speak further and just stared at her through the glass. *Crazy bitch*, Jasmine mumbled to herself as she shoved the key in the ignition. Her car purred to life.

She didn't know the specifics of what had happened to her mother after the airport incident fourteen months ago. But sending her fucking minion to call and pop up on her meant that wherever the hell Jayla was, she was alive and well. That alone was enough motivation for Jasmine to stay as far away from Patricia as possible. She was still hurt from the shit that had gone down, but she had moved on. She was trying to reestablish herself, and she had plans of her own. The fact that Jayla had had a sudden change of heart, wanting to reconcile and shit, meant absolutely nothing. As far as Jasmine was concerned, both of them could kiss her pregnant ass, and if they thought they could keep fucking with her, they were in for a rude awakening.

Jasmine was so busy fishing her cell phone from her purse that she didn't notice Patricia in the rearview mirror, her own cell phone to her ear, her eyes trained on the vehicle as she spoke to someone with a slight smirk on her face.

CHAPTER THREE

Jayla

Jayla awoke to the brief banging on her door, which was followed by the sound of the locks sliding out of place. She squinted at the strip of light underneath the door and watched the shadows cast by feet shuffling on the other side. With the exception of that strip of light, the isolation room was completely dark. It had taken Jayla a few days, or what she assumed had been a few days, to get used to the darkness. But eventually, her eyes had been able to make out the silhouette of the cot, the toilet, and the sink. She fucking hated solitary confinement, but she would be damned if she gave Banks the satisfaction of going crazy in the hole. So, she had slept mostly. And plotted.

The door swung open, and Jayla winced as the piercing light stung her eyes. She threw her hand up to block it and immediately felt a hand grab her wrist and yank her up from the cot.

"Let's go." The guard was one she had never seen before, but then again, she had managed until now to keep herself from landing on this side of the jail.

The guard clamped the steel cuffs on her wrists and pulled her along by her arm. Jayla stumbled, squinting, down the empty corridor lined with the doors of isolation cells. She wondered where Dreena was.

"How long was I in there?" she asked, her voice low and raspy.

"Three days," the guard said. "Would've been in there longer if your lucky ass wasn't getting out of here."

Jayla frowned and blinked as she was led through the empty recreation room. She knew she hadn't heard correctly. "Wait, what?"

"I said you would've been in there longer, like your girl Dreena. Technically, y'all both were supposed to do six weeks in the hole. But the warden sent down your discharge papers."

The hell? Jayla blinked again, struggling to process the information. That couldn't be right. She still had four months on her sentence. She opened her mouth to speak, but not wanting to fuck up whatever mistake she knew the jail had made, she shut it again.

The guard led her to an office and retrieved the clothes Jayla was wearing when she was brought in. Then she steered Jayla to the showers and told her to get cleaned up and to dress in her street clothes. Jayla hurriedly did as she was told. If all of this was real, she wanted out before they had an opportunity to change their minds. Once Jayla was dressed, a few inmates watched her curiously as she followed the guard back through the common area, through a few routine checkpoints, and toward the lobby.

Sure enough, her name had been written on a stack of release papers on one of the desks in the lobby. Either shock or confusion had Jayla scribbling her name wherever the woman behind the desk pointed. Her excitement was bubbling up, but she struggled to remain calm as the woman handed over the few personal items Jayla had come in with.

"All right, Ms. Morgan," the woman said with a smile. "You're free to go. Don't let us catch you back here."

Jayla slipped her purse on her shoulder and nodded. She turned and pushed through the glass door that led outside.

The sun shone brilliantly, and Jayla took a deep breath. The fresh air felt so pure she wanted to cry. No more did she have to worry about someone telling her when to get up, when to go to bed, when to eat, when to play, or hell, even when to change her fucking tampons. She didn't realize how much she had taken her freedom for granted before.

"Puma!"

Jayla grinned when she spotted Patricia leaning aga-inst a glistening black stretch limo parked alongside the curb. The woman looked just as refreshing in her tight pencil skirt and billowing green blouse. She stood up straight as Jayla walked over. Jayla threw her arms around her and noticed that Patricia smelled just as appetizing as she looked. Relishing the familiar embrace, she nuzzled Patricia's neck and felt her kitty purr in response.

Patricia pulled back and planted a delicious kiss on Jayla's lips before slipping her tongue in to massage Jayla's.

Jayla moaned from the kiss. "I've missed you," she murmured against Patricia's lips.

"I've missed you too, Puma," Patricia said. She stepped back and opened one of the back doors to the limo.

Jayla slid onto the crisp leather seat and exhaled. Her body was craving real food, wine, a bath, and definitely Patricia's sexy body. Patricia slipped into the limo's back seat right behind her, and Jayla leaned in to kiss her, then moaned as Patricia's tongue assaulted hers. She felt her pussy heating up from desire, and she spread her thighs, the need for Patricia's touch damn near bringing her to tears. To her surprise, Patricia broke the kiss and rested her hand on Jayla's shoulder.

"Puma, we can't," she said.

"What? Why?" Jayla's breath was ragged. "I've missed you."

"I've missed you too, but . . ." Patricia sighed and dropped her eyes. "It's complicated right now, and I promise to tell you when the time is right."

Jayla sat back in confusion. She was aching so bad, her body had started trembling. She could nearly taste the orgasm, because it was so close. And judging from Patricia's lust-filled eyes, she wanted it just as bad. So, what was wrong? Patricia had never rejected her before, and now she sat looking everywhere but at Jayla, as if she dreaded revealing whatever was on her mind. It was clear something was going on, but instead of revealing what it was, Patricia handed her a glass of champagne.

"I'm sure you need this," she said, masking her discomfort with a light laugh.

Grateful for the champagne, Jayla knocked back the liquid and damn near melted as it soothed her throat. Her head began hum, and she suddenly felt relaxed. "How did you do it?" she asked.

Patricia smiled. "I didn't. Sheila Weston did."

"Who?"

"You know Sheila Weston? Wife of Senator Grant Weston?"

Jayla paused as she struggled to put faces to the names. She vaguely remembered seeing the dynamic couple on TV and in magazines.

"Remember, I told you I knew someone who has a job for you?" Patricia reminded her.

Jayla groaned and rolled her eyes. "Yeah, and I remember telling you I wasn't interested."

Patricia smirked and took a sip of her own champagne. "Well, she pulled a shitload of strings to get you out so you could meet with her today. If I were you, I would be interested in what she has to say."

Jayla frowned but remained quiet. The atmosphere in the limo had suddenly grown tense. And she didn't know why, but she had a bad feeling about this prospective assignment.

The limo pulled into the parking lot of a marina, and Jayla glanced out at the yachts of various sizes and colors that were tied up on each side of the nearest wooden dock. Patricia gave her directions to a yacht called *Empress Weston* and insisted on waiting for her in the parking lot, which was probably for the best. Jayla didn't want to hear her mouth when she declined whatever this new assignment was.

The distinct smell of salt water hung in the air as Jayla climbed out of the limo. After shutting the limo door, she made her way through the maze of yachts to a large slip on the far side of the marina. The words *Empress Weston* were painted eloquently on the boat's bow, and without a moment's hesitation, Jayla stepped aboard. She found herself on a pristine deck and gazed around. Her eyes found Sheila, who was reclining in the plush seating area near the stern. She wore a skimpy yellow bikini that showed off her golden-bronze skin. Her almond-shaped eyes, set slightly wide apart, turned to Jayla, and she flashed a brilliant smile as Jayla made her way across the deck and then aft. When Jayla reached her, Sheila didn't bother rising from her perch and instead gestured with her glass toward the empty lounge chair across from her.

"Please have a seat," she said. "Can I get you something from the bar?"

Obediently, Jayla sat down. "No, thank you."

"Come on now. I know you need something after a year in jail." Sheila seemed to smirk at her statement as she put her own glass to her lips. She took her time polishing off the drink before she leaned over and sat the glass on a nearby table.

Jayla watched her silently. There was something about this woman that made her flesh crawl. She wished she would hurry up with whatever she needed to say.

"I'm not going to beat around the bush with you," Sheila began as she reached for a nearby pack of cigarettes. "I brought you here because I need to take down my husband." She pulled a cigarette from the pack.

Jayla lifted an eyebrow. “Your husband? *The* Grant Weston?”

“That’s the one.” Sheila lit the cigarette, puffed on it, and puckered her lips to blow out a steady stream of smoke. “I hear you’re good.”

Jayla’s mind flashed to Lauren and Marcus’s crazy ass hemming her up in her bedroom. Damn right she was good. She had almost been killed for it. It had taken months of counseling while incarcerated to stop the nightmares.

“Listen,” Sheila went on while Jayla remained silent. “It’s quite simple. I need an appraiser. My husband is a lying, conniving, cheating asshole who thinks just because he has a few dollars in the bank, he can do whatever the fuck he wants to do. I want to expose him.”

“Is that so?” Jayla didn’t bother hiding her suspicious frown. “So, this is not about money? Or some kind of prenup?”

Sheila took another deep pull from her cigarette and smiled at Jayla through the haze. “I said you were good,” she murmured, licking her lips. “Yes, money is part of it. Not only am I a greedy bitch, but I also feel I deserve every damn dime. I’ve put up with a lot of his shit. We have been together for seventeen years. Married for nine. I’m not going to act like money is not a factor. But more than money . . .” She paused. Lowering her voice for effect, she added, “I want to drag his ass through the gutta.”

Jayla saw something flick in her eyes. She couldn't tell if the woman was gloating or was a fucking lunatic. All she knew was that there appeared to be more to this situation than Mrs. Sheila Weston was letting on. And she damn sure didn't want to be part of it.

Jayla stood to go, an apologetic smile plastered on her lips. "I do appreciate the offer, Sheila. I do. But I'm going to have to respectfully decline."

Sheila sighed. "I am very generous, Ms. Morgan." She opened a drawer under the side table and pulled out a check.

Jayla's eyes lowered to the slip of paper as Sheila held it out. Two hundred fifty thousand dollars. Her breath caught as she reread the figure.

"Half now," Sheila was saying. "Half in a month."

"A month?"

"Yes. That's how long it should take. Plus, it's about time for elections, and I want to get this handled before he is reelected into office."

The unrealistic deadline had Jayla shaking her head. She hadn't even done a full assessment. Aside from the media's subjective portrayal of him, she didn't know anything about this man.

"Again, I'm sorry. I do appreciate the offer. Even if I did do it, there is no way I could finish in a month."

Sheila's lips dropped a few degrees, but she managed to keep her phony smile in place. She stood now, with the check still extended between them. "No, *I'm* sorry," she said, stepping closer. "Maybe I haven't made myself completely clear. You will do it, and you will have my evidence in four weeks. Do I make myself clear?"

Anger had Jayla's eyes glossing over. She was tempted to slam this uppity bitch into the railing of this little boat. And if her rational side didn't think she would be violating some sort of post-incarceration etiquette, she damn sure would. Either way, she knew she needed to leave, or it was about to be straight WorldStar, the Seaside edition.

Jayla turned and headed across the deck, then stopped abruptly when she heard the woman's light chuckle. She faced her once more. "What the hell is your problem? You really think you got enough money to force me to do something? Bitch, you tried it. That shit don't impress me."

"Bitch, please." Sheila was clearly amused. "I'm laughing because you really think your ho ass has a fucking choice." She flicked her cigarette over the side of the boat as she bit off each word. "The money is an incentive. Not a door for negotiation. Don't forget who got you out of jail. Fuck with me if you want to. The Weston name holds weight. I'll have you back behind bars before you even set foot on the dock. Maybe even transferred to some slum-ass prison. You'll be wondering why you're doing a ten-year sentence on a flimsy misdemeanor."

Jayla froze, the severity of the threat sending a bolt of fear shooting up her spine.

"You want to try me?" Sheila taunted Jayla, who remained silent. "I seriously doubt you do." She held the check out once more. "Welcome aboard, Ms. Morgan. I look forward to working with you."

Jayla walked back across the deck and took the check. The piece of paper felt dirty between her fingers. Sheila had the power. That much was true. Maybe, just maybe, it wouldn't hurt to use that to her advantage. Jayla smiled, even as her mind was already working in overdrive to sort out the details of a plan.

CHAPTER FOUR

Jasmine

"So where is your boo?" Kendra stepped through the sliding glass door, two wineglasses in hand.

Jasmine sighed as she accepted one of the glasses. "Probably with his wife," she admitted with a nonchalant shrug.

"*Ooh*, bitch, you so wrong."

Jasmine smirked. She knew she was, but she damn sure didn't care. She shifted uncomfortably on the chaise lounge and winced at the dull ache in her abdomen.

Kendra frowned upon noticing her best friend's discomfort. "What's wrong?"

"Nothing."

"I'm a CNA, Jazz. You can't lie to me." Kendra tugged on the pea-green hospital scrubs she wore from work. "Now, what's wrong with the baby?" she asked as she lay down on the chaise lounge next to Jasmine's.

"I said nothing. The doctor just said I need to take it easy."

"Get off from under that married boyfriend of yours and maybe you could take it easy." Kendra smirked into her glass.

Jasmine forced a weak grin. She wished it were that simple.

They lay there in silence for a while, listening to the distant hum of suburban traffic.

"Girl, I am loving this house, though," Kendra mused, kicking off her Crocs and folding her legs under her on the chaise.

"It's from Mister."

Kendra frowned. "I haven't heard you mention him in a while. Didn't know your sugar daddy was still around."

"Of course he is. I ain't got no job. I have to keep him in my back pocket." Jasmine gestured to the two-story brick condo as she spoke. The luxury residence, complete with the Bentley in her garage and the saltwater pool they were now lounging beside, was in a gated community. The gift had set him back, but as long as he played his position, she would play hers. And for now, she was his sugar baby, his trophy, his companion. It came with its perks, which was why she wouldn't let him go.

"I'm telling you," Jasmine went on, "you need to get you one and stop messing with these broke-ass dudes that can't do shit for you."

"Girl, stop." Kendra dismissed the comment with a wave of her hand. "I like my job. Besides, I'm scouting the hospital for a doctor husband. Just give me a few more months. I got my eye on a surgeon." She winked and giggled.

The phone rang from somewhere in the house, and Kendra went to retrieve it.

Jasmine sighed, looking out at the glistening pool and massaging the taut skin on her stomach. Worry masked her face. She hadn't felt the baby move in days, and the pain was becoming more and more frequent. She couldn't go back to the doctor. It would be too real if the ob-gyn verbalized what she thought she knew. She couldn't let that happen. Not to her. Or her boyfriend. She needed this baby. It was so much easier to remain hopeful.

"Oh, absolutely." Kendra was laughing on the phone as she made her way back outside. "I will surely tell her. Nice talking to you." She held the phone out. "It's your mom."

Jasmine rolled her eyes as she took the phone. She had been avoiding Jackie for days. As far as she was concerned, she didn't have to keep lying to her if she never spoke to her.

"Hey, Ma."

"I guess you get back out to school and forget you've got a family, huh?" Jackie said. "I've been trying to call you for a month. Why haven't I been able to reach you? Is something wrong?"

"I'm sorry. I've just been busy with school." The lie came naturally. But truth be told, she had dropped out when she had teamed up with Jayla as an appraiser. Then, when that money had run out, she had lucked up and met a sugar daddy on a little dating website. She didn't want or need for anything, so to hell with school.

"I'm glad you're focused on school," Jackie said. "But still. You know I worry about you. I don't talk to you for months at a time. Then, when I do talk to you, you're very short or always rushing me off the phone."

Jasmine didn't respond at first. Her relationship with Jackie had become strained over the past few months. She still felt anger and bitterness because the woman she loved and trusted had kept the ultimate secret from her. The news that Jayla, not Jackie, was her biological mother was still fucking with her psyche.

"How is Dad?" Jasmine finally said.

Jackie's sigh was heavy. "You know me and your dad are going through some things right now."

"Yeah?"

"Yeah. It's serious. I put him out."

"Damn. For real?" Jasmine winced, remembering whom she was talking to. "Sorry. But seriously? You put him out? What did he do?"

Jackie was silent for a moment. "It's a long story. But I just wanted you to hear it from me first."

"Dang, Ma." Jasmine shook her head, digesting the recent news. Damn, her dad must have fucked all the way up. She had never known her parents even to sleep in separate rooms. Let alone in separate houses. "You think this is just a temporary thing? Or . . ."

"No, this is probably permanent." Jackie's response was quick and definite. She sighed again. "Well, I'll let you go. I'm not trying to interrupt, but I just wanted to tell you that. I'm in a wedding, so we got to go do this dress-fitting thing."

"Fun. All right. Talk to you later."

"I love you, Jasmine."

Jasmine hung up the phone. She looked up to see that Kendra had stripped naked and her bronze skin was piercing the water as she did laps around the pool. She smirked. "Bitch, get yo' naked ass outa my pool," she said. "Don't nobody want your cunt juices all in my water."

Kendra laughed as she rested her arms on the marble pool deck. "Don't be jealous. By the way, your mom is hella cool. I thought you said y'all were close."

"We were." Jasmine swung her legs over the side of the chaise lounge, braced against the pain, and rose to her feet. "I'm going to go use the bathroom and make a phone call to the boo."

Kendra grinned. "Which one?"

“Mister is out of town for a few days, but I got someone to keep me company.” Jasmine winked as she wobbled toward the house.

It took every ounce of energy she had, but she finally made it upstairs to her bathroom. She could feel a small pool of liquid at the crotch of her panties and trickling down her leg. Ignoring the rise of panic within her, Jasmine grabbed a towel to clean herself up. She changed into a fresh pair of underwear, and for good measure, she put in a tampon. She willed herself to stay positive. She had to.

Jasmine remembered the note she had torn up from the one therapy session she had attended last year. *Clinical depression and borderline personality disorder*. They had been quick to diagnose her and suggest all these medications, but Jasmine had never gone back. She had been juggling a lot, and damned if it hadn’t stressed her out. But they’d wanted to slap a label of mental issues to justify her reaction to the bullshit she had gone through. Anything to make money.

Tears stung her eyes, and Jasmine turned from her sad reflection in the bathroom cabinet mirror. What she needed was a drink. She needed to get her shit together, because she could feel everything beginning to unravel. And she just couldn’t let that happen. She pulled open the mirror to expose the cabinet shelves behind it. The shelves were littered with medicine bottles, razors, eyedrops, Band-Aids, and extra toothpaste. She grabbed one of the pill bottles, and after shaking a tablet into her hand, she tossed it in her mouth and leaned under the faucet to wash it down with warm tap water.

The phone rang just then, and Jasmine wiped her damp cheeks as she crossed into the adjoining bedroom. She had tossed her cell phone on the bed when she first came upstairs. After snatching it from the sheets, she instantly smiled as a name flashed across the screen. She didn't care if he had a wife. She didn't care who judged her. All she knew was this man loved her and made her feel special. He was what she needed.

Jasmine clicked the phone on and placed it to her ear. "Hey, Marcus," she cooed. "When you coming to see me, baby?"

CHAPTER FIVE

Jayla

It felt damn good being back in his arms.

Jayla lay naked on Quentin's chest, her leg thrown across his lap, so her pussy lips kissed his hairy thigh. Their lovemaking had been intense, and even now, they lay on the cum-soaked sheets, because neither one had wanted to move.

Quentin had picked up a little weight, and the sprinkle of bumps on his face was evidence his skin had seen one too many razors. But other than that, he still looked pretty much the same, with his peanut butter complexion and his jet-black eyes, which he always kept halfway hidden under the dip of his eyelids. His sexy look, he called it. Jayla had to admit that though he was no Derrick, he was sexy enough. He had been her first love. She hadn't meant to fall in love with her sister's boyfriend as a teenager, and even after he and Jackie had got married, a piece of Jayla's heart had still belonged to him.

"You still got it, Jaye," Quentin murmured, his breath warm against her temple.

Jayla kept her eyes closed as her lips curled at his comment. "A far cry from when I was fourteen."

"Damn right."

She chuckled, listening to his heart beat against his chest. "You never told me why you moved out, Que." When he didn't respond, Jayla lifted her head and struggled to make out his facial features in the darkened room.

"To be honest," he said, "I've been thinking more and more about us. These past few months you've been locked up . . . I think it did something to me."

Jayla's heart picked up speed. "What did you tell Jackie?"

"I told her the truth. That I was having feelings for someone else. Of course, she was pissed. She found out we had been writing each other. I think she saw one of your letters or something. She never said anything, but she probably figured out it was you."

Jayla groaned and sat up, letting the sheets pool at her waist. Damn. Jackie was probably gonna try to fight next time she saw her. She swallowed, listening to Quentin's heavy breathing. Part of her didn't want to believe what he was intimating. "What are you saying, Que?"

He sat up as well, then angled his body so that she could lean her back on his chest. He touched his lips to her shoulder. "I'm saying that I loved your sister. But you have always been my number one."

"Wow." The word hung suspended between them as Jayla struggled to think of how else to respond. She had feelings for Quentin. That she couldn't deny. But she didn't know if she was prepared to be anything more than a fuck buddy. He had been there for her while she was in jail, but they had already crossed the line and gone as far as she was willing to go. And now he had left her sister to be with her?

She felt his fingers caressing her back, and she tossed a small smile over her shoulder. As awkward as the thought was in this situation, Derrick crossed her mind. How badly she had loved him, how desperately she had wanted to make a life with him. And ultimately, how badly she had hurt him, because she had been neck deep in deception with her Heartbreaker business. And now, considering she had to do this one final assignment to fulfill a debt, she would do it differently this time. She needed to focus and not pull anyone else into their feelings until she had completely severed herself from that lifestyle.

"Well?" Quentin prompted when Jayla had made no move to speak. "You know I've always loved you, girl. We got history."

"Que"—Jayla slid from the bed, pulling the sheet around her body—"you're still married to my sister. Last time we took off trying to explore some shit, I turned up pregnant. Not only that, but I caught feelings for you, too, so it hurt like hell when you went along with the marriage, but I had nobody to blame but myself." Jayla sighed with the weight of the admission. "Let's not complicate this right now."

Dejection creased his face, but Quentin nodded anyway. "You're right. Timing is bad. How about we talk about this again after my divorce?"

"Divorce?" Jayla's eyes ballooned. "You said you were taking a break. You didn't say you were getting a divorce."

Quentin gave a half-hearted shrug. "Yeah. It's just not working out between us. Shit's been fucked up for a long time, but we just been trying to hang in there."

The guilt felt like it was smothering her. "Damn," she murmured. Jayla turned, walked into the bathroom, and shut the door behind her. The news had a headache brewing right behind her eyes, so she reached for the mirror on the medicine cabinet and pulled it open. She needed something to relieve the pain.

Jayla's eyes scanned past the familiar bottle so fast, she had to do a double take. She frowned as she pulled the medicine from the cabinet to make sure her eyes weren't playing tricks on her. Anger had her vision blurring, so she could barely make out the harsh letters etched on the label. She took a deep breath to calm herself down. And the name of the drug on the label came into focus, clear as day. Atripla. They had prescribed her the same thing in jail. Which could mean only one thing.

"You son of a bitch!" Jayla screamed as she snatched open the bathroom door so hard the knob made a dent in the plaster.

Quentin looked up from his phone just in time to duck when she hurled the bottle at his head. "The fuck is wrong with you?"

"The fuck is wrong with me?" Jayla's head whipped around as she looked for something else to throw. "You didn't think to tell me, Quentin? Really?" She grabbed the remote and threw it at him. The device slammed into the wall and broke open, sending the batteries scattering. "Fuck you, you pussy-ass bitch! How long have you known you had HIV?"

Quentin frowned. "What?"

"Atripla, muthafucka?" Jayla swiped the tears burning her eyes. "How long, Quentin?" He lowered his eyes solemnly, and the realization that she was right had her chest tightening. "You knew you had it when you were with me. You fucking gave me HIV when I was fourteen."

"Jayla . . ." His voice was soft as his eyes met hers. He opened his mouth to speak again, but no words came out.

Jayla crumpled to the floor. She couldn't feel anything, and yet she felt every ounce of emotion as it surged like electric charges through her body. She had come to terms with her prognosis, blamed herself for the consequences of her scandalous exploits. But never would she have imagined that Quentin was the one who had signed her death certificate. Not her first love, Quentin, the man she had pretty much spoon-fed her virginity. She'd had the STD damn near all her life, and there was no telling how many people she had unknowingly infected. Numb, Jayla scrambled to her feet.

"Baby, I'm sorry," Quentin said helplessly. "I denied it for a long time. I was raped by my mother's friend as a teenager, and I struggled to put all of that out of my mind."

"But you knew." Jayla was in tears, her breath coming out jagged.

"Not at the time, I swear. I love you. I would've never done that to you. Jayla. Please listen to me." He had made his way to her, and now he grabbed her arms to stop her frantic movements. "I'm sorry. I should've told you when I first found out. I just didn't know how. Or even if I had passed it on to you."

"Well, you did." Jayla's voice cracked. "I found out last year."

"Shit . . . ," Quentin whispered, his hands falling limply to his sides. "Jayla . . . I . . . fuck . . . I am so sorry."

His helplessness infuriated Jayla. Before she knew it, her fist had snaked out and connected with his jaw. The impact had Quentin stumbling back a bit, but he didn't say a word.

"Go to hell, Quentin. I fucking hate your sorry ass." Jayla gathered up her things and ran from his apartment.

The drive to Patricia's was a blur. By the time Jayla braked in the driveway, she was exhausted from crying, and her head was pounding so hard that it felt like it was about to split open. Jayla sat in the SUV, eyeing Patricia's mini mansion through the windshield. It was funny how she had worked so hard for these same achievements. But at the cost of her life? And now she had just learned she had been damned as a teenager from the moment she pursued her older sister's boyfriend. Shit had been all downhill from there. Damn. Karma was a sneaky, backstabbing bitch in spiked stilettos.

Her phone chimed, signaling that she had an incoming text message. Jayla ignored the notification as she dragged herself from the car and headed inside.

Jayla's feet felt like lead as she pulled herself up the steps, opened the front door, and stepped inside. Patricia had left lights on for her inside the house, but she was nowhere to be found. Another chime on her phone and she swallowed a sigh. It was probably Quentin. She didn't know what he thought he could say to her now that would make any of this easier to digest. She needed someone to talk to.

Jayla headed down the hall toward Patricia's bedroom, noticed her door was closed, and paused a few feet from it. It was after two in the morning. She probably shouldn't wake her. Jayla turned to head to her own room. She didn't think she was prepared to have that conversation with Patricia anyway. Then they would have to address the elephant in the room. Had she given Patricia HIV? They had bumped and slurped coochies more times than she cared to remember. What would Patricia say when Jayla told her? *If* she told her?

Her phone chimed again, and aggravated, Jayla kicked the bedroom door closed and snatched the phone from her purse. She had been half right. The first text was from Quentin. Jayla, call me plz. It's important we talk more about this. I luv u. He could kiss her ass.

Jayla scrolled to Sheila's name and clicked the icon to begin a new message. Her fingers hovered over the keys for a brief moment before typing. I didn't realize who this was when you first told me. You are sure you want this done, right?

Sheila's response was quick, as if she had been waiting for the communication. Yes, I'm sure. Take care of it.

CHAPTER SIX

Jasmine

Jasmine ignored the throbbing pain as she continued to ride his dick like a prized stallion. She clenched her pussy muscles with each bounce, and her breath caught as he thrust his hips forward to meet her. She was sure the rough movement was tearing up something, but it was massaging her walls so good and he was groaning so loud, she couldn't bring herself to slow her speed.

"Oh, shit yeah." Marcus had his eyes closed as his fingers dug into her waist. "Fuck yeah, Jasmine. I love you, baby."

She grinned as the words played like a symphony to her ears. That was what she liked to hear. *Fuck that bitch Tracy.* Out of breath, Jasmine leaned forward and rested her huge stomach on his chest.

Marcus didn't break his momentum as he wrapped his arms around her back and squeezed her so tight she yelped in pain. He continued shoving all his inches in deep until a mixture of juices and blood coated his stiff shaft.

"Marcus," Jasmine whispered. Her kitty felt like it was on fire. "Marcus, baby—"

He gave one final thrust and emptied his nut into her. His breath roared in her ear and warmed her face as he lay back, exhausted from the orgasm.

Jasmine sighed. She loved being intimate with her man, but damn, if she wasn't glad this round was over. Her stomach was pressed tightly between their bodies, but she didn't want to move, relishing the feel of his arms around her.

"I love you, Marcus," she murmured. And she really did. He was the only man out of all the men she had dealt with who signified more than just sex to her. He made her feel complete. Her lips curved when she felt the kiss brush her forehead.

"I love you too," he said. "Have you given any more thought to what we talked about?"

Jasmine was glad it was dark, so he couldn't see her frown. For some reason, he had been pushing the issue about meeting her family. She didn't understand it, given their circumstances, and frankly, his persistence was riding her nerves.

"You know I'm not really close to my family, Marcus," she said. "That's why it's no big deal to me. I don't care whether they like you or not."

"Yeah, but I do. I told you how important that is for me if we're going to be together. You don't have some sort of family reunion or something coming up?"

"I don't know."

Marcus lifted her face up to meet his, and even though it was dark, Jasmine wiped the agitation from her face. "Can you look into it for me, baby?" he said. "Please?"

Jasmine knew she wouldn't, but she nodded anyway. The request was simple enough. So why the hell did it sound so suspect?

They lay there, sweaty, basking in the post-sex glow. As usual, Jasmine rubbed his muscular chest, and her fingers grazed the stiff skin around his bullet wound. The skin was rough, like leather healing. He had never given her too much detail about who had shot him, where, or why, and Jasmine had always noticed that he would get angry when she pressed him, so she eventually had stopped asking. She wondered if it was Tracy or one of the other hoes he probably had fucked with. Either way, she couldn't deny the sexy "bad boy" persona he had now, thanks to that permanent addition to his body.

Jasmine closed her eyes and listened to his rapid heartbeat slowly subside. Then his light snore echoed in the dark room. Jasmine giggled to herself. Like clockwork. Every time. Part of her wondered if Tracy, Marcus's wife, had him like this. Exhausted and drooling after some good pussy. She was tempted to be petty and send the bitch a picture. But Jasmine had just healed from the black eye Marcus had given her the last time she involved his wife. So, Jasmine just watched him sleep, wistfully playing the scene with Tracy in her head, if she were bold enough to try it. She liked to talk shit, but at the end of the day, she knew her position.

The ringing phone broke Jasmine's concentration, and she sucked her teeth. *Damn.* She didn't feel like talking to him, but that was Mister's ringtone, and he would be pissed if she didn't answer.

Jasmine maneuvered from Marcus's arms and reached for the phone on her nightstand. She cleared the sex from her voice before putting the phone to her ear. "Hey, Mister," she greeted.

"How's my girl?"

"Missing you so bad, Daddy."

"Aw, that's what I like to hear."

Jasmine shook her head, glancing absently at Marcus's body. She had this poor old man so far up her ass, it was a wonder she couldn't taste his shaving cream.

"I'm back in town," he was saying, "and wouldn't you know, I have this fundraiser thing to attend this evening. Everyone will be there, and I expect to see you there too."

Jasmine groaned inwardly. She had expected to lie up with Marcus all night. She was tired. And when Mister asked her to attend one of these boring-ass functions, it meant that for appearances, he had to ignore her as she pranced around in some skimpy dress, until he was able to sneak off and bend her over in the nearest bathroom or closet. Not really how she wanted to spend her evening, but she very well couldn't tell him that.

"I would love to," she said instead, feigning enthusiasm. "What time do you need Daddy's girl to be ready?"

"I'll come pick you up in two hours."

"I'll be waiting." Jasmine blew a kiss through the phone and hung up. She jumped, startled, when she heard Marcus sit up in the bed.

"Why you even still dealing with that nigga?" he snapped.

Jasmine rolled her eyes. *Here we go.* "Why you still dealing with Tracy?" she countered.

"Don't even trip, Jasmine. You know that's my wife. You know my situation, and you know I'm handling my shit." He paused, then pressed on when Jasmine remained quiet. "I'm just saying, now that you got me, you ain't got to be taking that nigga's money."

"We have an arrangement, Marcus," she reminded him, rolling her eyes. For some reason, he always seemed to forget that part unless it benefited him.

"See, here you go with that bullshit. I told you when you had my baby, we were gone be a family, right? I'm leaving Tracy."

Jasmine suddenly felt a sharp pain, which forced a moan from her lips.

Marcus reached out and placed his hand on her stomach. "What's wrong?"

"Nothing," she lied. "Probably gas."

Marcus's frown still hung on his face. He gently rubbed her bulging belly. "You not still fucking him, are you?" he asked.

Jasmine looked him dead in the eye, not missing a beat. "No," she lied again. She decided to follow up with the truth to ease his concern. "Baby, you know I love you, and everything I do is for you. For us." She touched his cheek and gave him a gentle kiss. "What is it? What's the problem? Why are we on this all of a sudden? You never made a big deal about him before."

"I know." Marcus sighed. "It's just . . . I'm worried as hell. Ever since Tracy lost the last child, I feel broken. She knew how much I wanted a kid. But damn! Three fucking miscarriages? I just can't take that shit. I don't know what the fuck is wrong with her fucked-up body, but she can't carry my kid, and I ain't getting no damn younger."

He had turned his back to Jasmine, and she took the liberty to rub it. "I know," she soothed. "I know it hurts. That's why you don't need her. You need me."

Marcus turned back around and kissed her. "We need this baby," he whispered, his eyes sharp on hers. "But I'm trusting you. That's why I'm still letting you kick it with ole dude. But I don't want you to fuck this up for us. Understand? You're carrying my seed. Don't make me regret being with you, Jasmine. Real talk."

The threat was subtle, but clear enough to send a chill up her spine. She knew the baby wasn't his, but she would slit her own throat before she told him that. Marcus had to have a low sperm count or something, because for whatever reason, the nigga had been shooting blanks. So, she had done what she had to do. But that didn't matter now. She was pregnant. That was what mattered. And as long as he didn't question the paternity, and she never gave him a reason to, they would be just fine.

Jasmine gave him a reassuring kiss, even as doubts about her baby's health flooded her mind. "I'm going to give you your baby," she promised.

Jasmine eyed herself in the full-length mirror, making sure the evening dress hid her baby bump. The royal-blue tunic dress had cap sleeves that fell elegantly off her shoulders. Her breasts had grown tremendously and spilled out over the crystal-embroidered sweetheart neckline. The dress draped over her belly, and one would have to be scrutinizing her figure closely to see the outlines of a stomach. *Good.*

Concealing her pregnancy from Mister had demanded a high level of creativity. Mister loved the sex, for sure. Jasmine made sure to rock his world so he would keep the gifts and money raining down on her. He was so eager to get between her thighs, he hadn't even commented when she started to leave her clothes on. And, by the off chance that he did want her naked, well, she just had to get a little clever. She'd keep the lights out. Use blindfolds. Keep his hands and mouth full. So far, she had pulled off keeping her clothes on, though a few times she had had to claim she was bloated. He hadn't asked any questions, and she hadn't volunteered any information. But she didn't know how much longer before he noticed. Or if he already had, how much longer he would pretend to ignore it.

Jasmine hadn't intended to get a sugar daddy. She hadn't known what to do after she cooperated with the police to send Jayla to jail. That Heartbreaker money had dried up quick, and with Jayla out of the picture, she didn't really know how to attract new clients while being under the police radar. She had gotten desperate. And sloppy.

One day she had gone into a clothing store to boost some shit to pawn, and she'd met this handsome and distinguished man in his early sixties. Having watched her place a few tagged items in her purse, he had assumed she needed clothes and had bought them for her. She'd looked on as he drop thirty-two hundred dollars on her like he was buying her some gum at the dollar store, and that had damn near made her cream right there at the register. She knew she needed to sink her hooks into this dude. So, she flirted with him and teased him the rest of the afternoon. She didn't realize until later that evening that this man was *the* Grant Weston. But knowing how long the senator's money ran damn sure didn't hurt either.

Their relationship was simple. Grant was looking to pay for companionship. Jasmine was looking for money. One year later Jasmine was still milking that cash cow. But ever since she had met Marcus, she'd known something would have to give. Eventually. She just didn't know if she was ready to let go of Grant. Or if he would even let her leave.

Jasmine heard the front door close and footsteps head up the stairs. She rushed to check herself in the mirror one last time. Since Grant had a key, she had to stay at the ready at all times.

"Where is Daddy's girl?" His voice flitted into the room first.

Jasmine turned just in time to see his body frame the doorway. She smiled. "Right here, Big Daddy."

One thing was for sure. If Grant wasn't forty years older than her, she may have considered something more with him. He looked damn good for his age: his skin was a rich brown like Godiva chocolate, and his piercing black eyes were a wonderful counterpoint to the black and gray of his hair and goatee. He was large compared to Jasmine, a full six feet, three inches in stature, and so she had to crane her neck to look him in his eyes. And he had the weight to match his height. He reminded Jasmine more of an athlete than a politician, but the man could wear the hell out of a suit.

As was customary, Jasmine ran into his outstretched arms, making sure to angle her body so as not to press her stomach into him. She lifted her face and welcomed the passionate kiss. Immediately, her tongue sought his, and she sucked on the plump flesh just like he liked it.

Grant moaned in response. When his hands moved to her legs to lift her dress, Jasmine pulled back. Her pussy was still sore from Marcus's brutal beating. She needed a break.

"What's the matter, baby girl?" His tone was disapproving.

Jasmine thought fast. "I just . . . have a craving. I'm so thirsty for your cum, and it's been so long since you've had that delicious dick in my mouth."

Grant seemed satisfied with the lie, and he leaned back and allowed Jasmine to undo the button of his Armani dress slacks.

Jasmine stooped to her knees and took him in her mouth, her lips wrapping around the thick shaft and coating it with spit. He was nowhere near as big as Marcus, but he was still satisfying just the same. So, she went to work, deep-throating every inch until her jaws locked. Even then, she continued to suck on the swollen tip like a pacifier. When he pulled out and lifted his leg on the nearby dresser, Jasmine knew exactly what he wanted her to do.

She had to admit, the thought of eating a nigga's ass had sickened her to no end. So, when he first made the request, she had refused. But knowing how to get her in the mood, he had given her a Dooney & Bourke tote, purse, and matching wallet stuffed with hundred-dollar bills. After that, she really hadn't been in a position to decline. It had been her first time, but apparently, she knew how to eat some damn groceries, because his requests had gradually become more and more frequent.

Jasmine licked his balls first, polishing each one like a prized pearl. She then worked her way back, parted his booty cheeks, and closed her lips around the rim of his hole. She focused on not thinking as she worked her tongue, sucking and lapping until her saliva was dripping from his crack. She ignored the smell, the feel of cheeks between her clenched fingers, and put her neck into the motion until she felt his legs tremble.

"Oh, fuck yes," he moaned. "That's it, baby girl. Just like that."

Ready to send him over the edge, Jasmine grabbed his dick and began jacking him off as she ate his ass inside out. It didn't take long before she felt it throbbing with the building orgasm and she heard his yell as his cum shot out, thick and creamy, and coated Jasmine's hand.

She sat back on her heels and looked up at Grant adoringly. "Can't you tell how much I missed you, Daddy?" she cooed. "I've been so lonely without you."

Grant chuckled as he leaned against the wall. "I can tell. You know how to make me feel so good."

"And you know I like making my Big Daddy feel good." Jasmine rose to her feet and crossed into her bathroom, struggling to keep the waddle out of her walk. She quickly washed her hands and brushed her teeth.

By the time she emerged, Grant was fully dressed again, waiting patiently on the bed. He held out his hand. "Baby girl, let me ask you something."

Jasmine let him pull her down on his lap. Her heart hit a backflip. She wondered what he could possibly have to say. She had long since noticed the tan lines from the wedding band he never wore around her, so she knew that couldn't be it. And he was much too calm to know about Marcus.

"You know I enjoy us," he began. "You give me everything I could ever want and more. I'm starting to have some serious feelings for you, baby girl."

Jasmine's breath caught as she listened, and she struggled to keep her face neutral. *Shit, shit, shit.* "Um . . ." She forced a smile. "Mister, you know how I feel about you. You mean everything to me. But why are you telling me this?"

Grant smiled as he ran a gentle finger down her cheek. He kissed her forehead. "We have to go," he said. "But we'll talk more about this another time. I just want you to know how I feel and that I'm starting to want more out of this relationship."

Jasmine cursed herself, wondering how she had managed to complicate their situation. Even as he held her hand and led her to the stairs so they could leave, she knew she needed to come up with something to get herself out of this mess. She had Grant in his feelings. A nigga in love, one with some deep pockets. Shit had just got real. And dangerous.

CHAPTER SEVEN

Jayla

"You have a collect call from . . ." The automated message paused long enough for the familiar voice to come on the line.

"It's me, girl."

Jayla shook her head with a grin at the sound of Dreena's voice. She maneuvered the car with one hand, remaining discreet as she tailed Grant's Lincoln Town Car. It braked at the curb in front of a jewelry store, and Jayla pulled over a block away and watched the driver get out and skirt the back of the car to open the passenger rear door nearest to the sidewalk.

"Press one to accept the charges. Press two to—"

Jayla punched a digit and put the phone to her ear while keeping her eyes trained on the car.

Grant emerged, followed by what appeared to be his security detail. He readjusted the lapels of his blazer and glanced around.

"Jayla?" Dreena's voice blared in her ear.

"Hey, what's up?"

Grant followed the security guys into the store, and Jayla shut her car off. Now was as good a time as any.

"Bitch, that was some real foul shit you pulled," Dreena snarled.

Jayla frowned at the woman's harsh tone. "What are you—"

"Don't play fucking retarded!" Dreena yelled. "You set me up to take the fall for that sex shit we was doing in here."

"No, I didn't, Dreena. Who said that?"

"Banks dropped the dime on you."

"Banks?" Jayla scoffed, remembering the conniving security guard from jail. "I told you she had it in for me. She's fucking lying."

"Maybe she is. Maybe she isn't," Dreena growled. "But it's just mighty funny how they peg both of us for that shit, we're thrown in the hole, and then your ass is being served some walking papers a few days later. Now explain that shit."

Jayla sighed, rubbing her eyes. "It's complicated. But I know some folks."

"You a pussy-ass liar," Dreena yelled. "It's so fucking convenient how after that, you get a muhfucking get-outa-jail-free card and they hemming my ass up in the hole for weeks. And adding time on my sentence."

"That's fucked up, Dreena, but I ain't did nothing." Jayla's voice was laced with aggravation. Why was she up here explaining anything to this bitch? They weren't even friends like that. Dreena was just some chick she knew to keep bitches off her ass while she was locked up.

Dreena was rambling. "Fuck that," she said. "I know people, too, so you betta watch your backstabbing back. Karma is a muhfucka, and when I get out—"

Jayla hung up, rolling her eyes. She had more important things to handle, and Dreena's sensitive ass was not one of them. This was her business, and Dreena wanted to whine because her ass was still behind bars. Hell, it wasn't a get-out-of-jail-free card that got her out of the big house. She was paying off a damn debt. And she was about to start making payments right now.

She stepped out of the car. Her tight black capris, black long-sleeve shirt with a plunging neckline, and red and gold pumps made it obvious that her body was begging for attention. The fabric of the capris and the shirt hugged her so tight that folks could probably see the freckles on her skin. Jayla's wig was all black and bone straight, and the razor-cut bangs lay on her forehead. She was looking edible, she knew, as she swished her ample ass across the street and into the jewelry store.

The interior of the store was a maze of glass cases, each featuring a selection of expensive rocks glittering from rings, necklaces, earrings, and bracelets. Some of the rocks were so brilliant that they cast rays of light across the paneled ceiling. Apparently, Grant's presence had emptied the store, because no one was there but him and his crew. Jayla watched him casually bend over one of the jewelry cases, his eyebrows furrowed as he thought, and she smiled. This would be too easy.

"Excuse me, miss." The voice stopped her short, and she struggled to keep from rolling her eyes at the man. "Ma'am, you can't be here."

"Oh. I apologize. Is the store closed or something?"

"No, ma'am, but—"

"Oh, okay. Well, I am just needing to get a birthday gift for my sister really quick." She flashed a brilliant smile.

The man cleared his throat, and she saw his eyes slide behind her. "I apologize, ma'am, but—"

"Well, what's the problem?" Jayla lifted her voice to draw a bit more attention to herself. She threw up her hands to emphasize her impatience. "Do you work here or something? Am I bothering you in any way?"

"Carl." Grant's voice came from behind her, and she smiled inwardly. Grant's tone of voice had conveyed an understood command, and it had the guard nodding and stepping away.

Jayla turned to Grant, and her eyes glazed over with feigned excitement. "Are you Senator Weston?"

He chuckled lightly and held out his hand. "Pleasure to meet you . . ."

"Rochelle," she said, accepting the hand and giving it a flirty squeeze. "It's such an honor to meet you, sir. You've done a lot for our little community, and I have the utmost respect for your passion for helping others. Especially your work on approving the budget for the homeless center."

Grant's smile widened at the admiration. "Why, thank you, Ms. Rochelle."

"Please, sir. No *Ms*. Just Rochelle. I'm so sorry to disturb you while you're shopping." She made no move to remove her hand from his and instead took the opportunity to step closer to him. Grant cleared his throat, and she saw his internal struggle to keep from looking at her plump cleavage. Jayla slipped her hand from his, gently raking her nails along his palm as she performed the gesture.

Her eyes took a noticeable dive to the imprint in his pants. "So, can I help you with anything?" she said, licking her lips.

"Um . . ."

Jayla giggled and gestured toward the jewelry at his back. "Picking out jewelry. You look like you could use some help. Looking for something for someone special?"

Oh," he fumbled, laughing. "Uh . . . yeah. She is very special. My daughter." He turned and approached the jewelry case he had been perusing.

Jayla followed and stood beside him, entirely too close, and she smiled when he didn't move. She eyed the expensive pieces under consideration. "How about something like that?" she suggested, pointing. "It's simple but beautiful, and it says, 'Proud papa.'"

Grant nodded and gestured for the saleswoman to remove the item from the glass enclosure. Sure enough, the tennis bracelet, embellished with diamonds in a gold setting, was absolutely gorgeous. The woman started to launch into her pitch about cut and clarity, but Grant waved her off and instead looked to Jayla for confirmation. She nodded her approval with a smile.

"I'll take it," he said, and the saleswoman scurried off in excitement to ring up the expensive purchase. “Thank you,” he said. “You made that so easy.”

“I like to make things easy, Senator Weston,” she replied, flirting, as she fingered the collar of his blazer.

“Is that so?”

“Very much so.” Jayla licked her lips again and took her time stepping back. “You have to let me know the next time you have a general public function. Or you’re in the community, kissing babies, or whatever it is you politicians do.”

Grant laughed, obviously grateful for the break in the sexual tension. Shit was thick. “Will do.”

“Your office is over on the Northside of Atlanta, right? In Regions Plaza?”

“Sure is. Why? You going to be looking for me?”

Jayla smiled at his weak attempt at a joke. She gave a half shrug. “Maybe.”

“Um, excuse me, sir.” The guard from earlier, Carl, stepped between them. “I don’t mean to interrupt, but you have an important phone call.”

“Nice to meet you, Senator,” Jayla said, then gave him one last smile before walking off.

“You too, Rochelle.”

She felt his eyes on her as she walked back outside, and she couldn’t help but giggle. She still had it. She hated coming on to the man like some lovestruck groupie, but she needed to get the ball rolling. And fast. Sheila was getting impatient.

She was headed to her car when something stopped her dead in her tracks in the middle of the street. Jackie emerged from a restaurant, carrying a to-go bag. Her sister had cut her hair short and had picked up a little weight. She had easily surpassed thick on the scale and was now in the borderline fat range, filling out a pair of whitewashed jeans and a baby tee that accented her rolls.

Jayla was debating if she should approach her when the restaurant door swung open again and out stepped Tara. She gasped.

In sharp contrast to her companion, Tara looked gorgeous in her mini tube dress, which was cinched at the waist and billowed out to flirt with her knees. She had streaked her hair burgundy and swept it up in a casual bun, which highlighted her brilliant smile. Jackie had held the door open for Tara as she was pushing a stroller adorned with blue and green polka dots.

Jayla hadn't seen either of them in so long. Hell, she had forgotten Tara was even pregnant, the way she had beaten her ass that last time. Obviously, everything was going well for Tara, because she was definitely back to her prepregnancy weight.

The two exchanged a hug before Jackie stooped down and made a few kissy faces at the baby. Jayla frowned as she watched them part ways. What the hell was going on? Since when were they Oprah and Gayle? Of course, since Tara had been Jayla's best friend, she had always been around her family. But Jayla didn't remember ever seeing the two of them together without her. Something was definitely strange about that.

Curiosity fueled Jayla as she followed her sister to the parking lot. They hadn't spoken since Jackie had tried to splatter Jayla's ass in the middle of the interstate. Jackie hadn't even had the decency to see if Jayla was dead or alive after the incident, nor had she given two fucks about Jayla while she was locked up. Not even to tell her that her aunt Bev had died, which was downright coldhearted.

Jayla swallowed the swelling anger. She didn't want to fight her sister out here like a bitch in the street. But damn if she wasn't tempted.

"Jackie."

Jackie paused at her car and turned to eye her sister, who stood just a few feet away. A mirage of emotions played on her face. Her eyes darted to the restaurant.

She's probably wondering if I saw her with Tara, Jayla thought.

They stood still for a moment, neither sister speaking. Jayla remembered Jackie had found the letters she'd written to Quentin when she was in jail. She watched her anxiously, but Jackie's face remained surprisingly calm.

Jackie was the first to break the awkward silence. "When did you get out?"

Jayla scoffed. "So, you *did* know I was locked up!"

"Don't even try it." Jackie rolled her eyes at the sarcasm. "You act like we were on speaking terms. Of course I knew. But frankly, my dear, I didn't give a fuck. That's what your ass got." She turned to get in the car, as if that was the end of the conversation.

The bite of her words stung like hell. "So that's how it is now, Jackie? You just gone write me off as dead? Like Jocelyn?"

The mention of their sister halted Jackie's movements. Then she whirled around, and her chubby finger came within inches of Jayla's nose. "Don't you ever mention Jocelyn," she barked, the faint smell of wine on her breath. "It was your ratchet bullshit that got her killed."

"Damn, Jackie. What can I do? I made some mistakes. I had to marinate on that shit every day in jail. I have to live with it every day of my life.

Don't you think I feel guilty enough?" *Jocelyn, Derrick, HIV, Jasmine, hostage, death . . .*, she thought. "I'm suffering every day," Jayla added, her voice cracking, and she looked away to keep the tears from falling.

Jackie wasn't moved. A frown on her face, she eyed Jayla's raunchy attire. "Yeah, I can tell you are. They let you out and you back on the street corner already?"

"Dammit, Jackie! I get you're all in your feelings right now, but I will not stand here and let you keep disrespecting me."

"Really, bitch?" Jackie drew back, her face tightening with restrained anger of her own. "You disrespected your damn self. You tried to pimp my daughter, Jayla. You made her abort my grandchild. You've been prostituting for as long as I've known you, and it was your lifestyle that got our baby sister killed. What else is there?" she snarled, her eyes brimming with disgust as each word dropped from her lips.

Jayla glanced away. The loaded question was meant to be rhetorical, she knew. There was more, but the secrets Jackie had already spewed were damaging enough.

"I have every reason to hate you, Jayla," Jackie went on, her tone now carrying more sadness than anger. "I want to hate you. You destroyed everything."

"I feel that way about myself," Jayla admitted in a low voice.

"I don't know where you expect us to go from here. I really don't." Jackie sighed. Then she mumbled, "Talk to you later," got in the car, and closed the door.

Jayla didn't know if the words were sincere or if this was a generic goodbye, but either way, she stood back as the Cherokee sped off. She let out a heavy breath. Jackie was right. She didn't know what to expect either. Not given everything that had happened. But she would rather keep that door open for some unexpected possibility than not open it at all. Aside from Patricia, Jackie was the only family she had. Especially now that Aunt Bev was gone.

"That was so touching."

The cynical voice startled Jayla, and she whipped around to see Sheila leaning against the hood of a sleek black Range Rover, a cigarette bobbing at the corner of her upturned lips.

"What the fuck, Sheila?" Jayla snapped. "What are you doing here? Are you following me?"

Sheila smirked, lifting her shoulder in a nonchalant shrug. Her silence was admission enough. "I'm just making sure I'm getting my money's worth." She used her manicured nail to tap on the face of her watch. "Time is money, and you look as if you're wasting it. Which means I'm not happy."

Jayla frowned. Sheila was acting like her pimp. All she needed was a damn hat and a pinkie ring. "I don't need to be micromanaged. You need me, remember?'

Sheila chuckled as she blew out smoke. Though she still had half a stick left, she flicked the cigarette onto the blacktop. "Last I checked, you need me just as much. But don't worry. I'm going to let you do your thing. I actually came to talk to you about something else."

"What is it?"

A hint of worry had Sheila's face shifting a bit. She glanced around before lowering her voice and saying, "We have a problem."

CHAPTER EIGHT

Jasmine

Jasmine had barely made it to the toilet before she collapsed to her knees and threw up for the fourth time. It felt like her insides were threatening to come up, and the stomach acid was singeing her throat as she coughed and gagged.

She sniffed, wiping the sweat matting her hair to her forehead. The gesture made her palm feel hot, and she knew she still had a fever. Especially considering she was shivering from chills, despite the fact that her T-shirt was clinging to her wet skin.

Weak, Jasmine crawled back into her bedroom. Squinting through a film of sweat and tears, she was able to make out the impression of the phone on the bed. She fumbled for it, dry heaving, and wiped away the dribble from her lips. All she could think about was her baby as her fingers trembled over each digit on the phone's keypad.

Just like the other times, Marcus's phone went straight to voicemail. She didn't even have the energy to leave a message, so Jasmine hung up. She dialed another number and prayed like hell she would get an answer.

"Hello?" Kendra's voice was barely audible over the noise in the background.

"Kendra. Help me." Exhaustion had her voice coming out in a whisper, and Jasmine swallowed again, feeling another bout of nausea swelling up from her stomach.

"Jazz, is that you? I can't hear you."

"Kendra, please . . ."

"Jasmine? Hello?" Kendra was yelling now.

The phone slipped from Jasmine's limp fingers as she collapsed, enveloped in fear and darkness.

Jasmine awoke feeling groggy and disoriented. Vomit aftertaste coated her mouth, and there was a dull ache near her lower abdomen. Her body felt stiff and weak. She struggled to open her eyes with a groan.

"Jazz?"

Jasmine groaned again and turned her head in the direction of Kendra's voice.

"Don't move," Kendra said. "I'll get the doctor."

"No." Jasmine's own voice was so hoarse, she barely recognized it. She managed to open her eyes, and her vision was cloudy before the room came into focus.

A hospital room. She was hooked up to all kinds of noisy machines, and when she shifted, she felt the pinch of the needle from the IV drip in her arm. Kendra stood at her bedside, her eyes large with worry.

"You okay?" she asked.

"Yeah. What happened?" Then the memory of her sickness flooded back with such intensity that it gave her a little strength. "My baby?"

"Bitch, if you weren't in that damn bed, I would kill you." Kendra's voice conveyed her relief, despite the threat. "You scared the shit outa me."

"What happened?"

"I got a call from you. You were mumbling something before the phone went dead. I was worried as hell, Jasmine. I kept calling you back, but the phone kept going to voicemail, so I'm panicking, like, 'Shit! What's wrong? What happened?' So, I come over, and I'm scaling the fucking fence like Catwoman and breaking through your patio door, because you couldn't answer the door." Kendra's voice quivered as she spoke, and Jasmine dropped her eyes.

"I'm sorry," she murmured.

"There was so much blood and throw-up, Jasmine. You were passed out in the middle of the floor. I called the ambulance and rushed here with you to the hospital. You almost died."

"My baby?"

Kendra looked up, struggling to keep the tears from falling. "The baby had been dead. The doctor said for a few months now. That's why you were sick. Apparently, you got some kind of infection. Blood clots and everything. They did an emergency C-section. It's been touch and go ever since."

Jasmine closed her eyes, letting the tears streak down her pale cheeks. She had tried to save her baby. What was she going to tell Marcus?

"Jasmine . . ." Kendra's voice was cautious. "How long have you known you have HIV?"

Jasmine felt her face heat with embarrassment. "I . . . when I got pregnant." She meant when she got pregnant the first time, and Jayla had made her have an abortion, but she wouldn't tell that to Kendra. Some things she just didn't need to know.

Kendra's sigh was heavy. "Do you know who you got it from?"

Jasmine felt the tears on her eyelashes, and she shook her head. The doctors had guessed she had been infected with HIV for a while, but there was no way to know for sure. And she had slept around . . . a lot. It could've been anybody. She felt Kendra place her hand on her arm and give it a comforting squeeze.

"Jasmine, none of that matters," Kendra went on. "I'm so sorry, but with everything you went through, I'm just so glad you're alive. Damn, girl. Shit was bad. Did you know the baby was dead?"

Jasmine couldn't bring herself to speak the lie to her best friend, so she just shook her head.

"I'm sorry. Do you need me to get the doctor? Are you in pain?"

"Where is my phone?"

"Back at the house. Here." Kendra pulled her own cell phone from her pocket and handed it over.

Jasmine dialed Marcus again and was pissed when the phone went right to voicemail. "Oh, is that how we do, Marcus?" she snapped, leaving a message. "You get tired of my calls and cut your fucking phone off? What's the matter? Don't want your wife knowing what's going on? Fuck that, you pussy muthafucka. Bring your ass to Northside Hospital now. I'm down here, sick because of your child, dammit. I could kill your ass for making me go through this alone. Stop being a bitch, Marcus!" Jasmine hung up and sighed in frustration. Just when she needed him the most, he wanted to be

Cliff fucking Huxtable and treat her like the side piece.

She handed the phone back to Kendra. “Thanks, girl.”

“Call the other one. Mister.”

“I can’t. He doesn’t know I’m pregnant.” *Not to mention his precious image. He would kill me if it ever comes out that the baby was his.*

Kendra watched helplessly as Jasmine broke into another fit of sobs. She knew about her friend’s mental disorder. She had accompanied her to the therapist session. And she knew Jasmine’s fragility from something this traumatic could destroy her.

Jasmine was sick again from refusing to eat. Her baby’s death was all but eating her alive. Not to mention Marcus still had not returned her calls.

By day three, Kendra was fed up. “So, you just going to sit in here and die?” she fumed, snatching open the flimsy window curtains.

Jasmine winced when the glaring sunlight spilled into the hospital room. Her tear-streaked face was solemn as she watched Kendra yell and pace the room.

“I really don’t get you,” she rambled on. “I’m trying to be there for you, but your ass needs to see a damn therapist.”

The words hurt, but Jasmine didn't bother responding. She looked toward the window, wishing she were somewhere else. Anywhere else but here. She knew she looked as bad as she felt. She had lost so much weight, her hospital gown swallowed her. Dark circles outlined her sunken eyes, and she hadn't bothered to fix the tangled weave that was now matted to her scalp. She wished the annoying staff, including Kendra, would just leave her to die in peace.

"*Hello*. Jasmine, snap out of it!" Kendra snapped her fingers for emphasis. "What is it going to take, Jasmine? Call your boyfriend. Call Mister. Hell, call your mom. Call somebody. Between working up here and coming to spend time with you every night and every break, it's really wearing me out."

"Then leave me alone," Jasmine said.

Kendra sighed, suddenly feeling guilty. She rested a hip on the edge of the bed and laid her hand on Jasmine's frail leg. "I'm sorry. But, damn, I'm worried about you, Jazz. Talk to me. What can I do?"

Jasmine closed her eyes as fresh tears dampened her cheeks. "I need my baby," she whispered. She felt the bed shift as Kendra stood.

"I love you, Jazz. You're like a sister to me. I hate seeing you like this." Her eyes lifted to the clock on the wall, and she sighed. "I got to get back downstairs to work. I'm pulling a twelve-hour rotation, but I'll come see you on my next break. Okay?" When Jasmine didn't respond, Kendra turned and headed toward the door.

Jasmine held her breath as she opened her mouth to speak. The thought had crossed her mind, but the more she had dwelled on it, the more it had consumed her. She just had to ask. Even if the brazen request destroyed their relationship.

"Kendra? Can you do me a favor?"

Her friend stopped at the door and turned to look at her. "Anything, Jazz. What is it?"

Jasmine looked at her friend. Her eyes felt so heavy. "Can you bring me a baby from the nursery?"

Kendra frowned. "What?"

"Can you bring me—"

"I heard what you said," she hissed, looking over her shoulder, as if someone else had heard the question. She stepped closer. "What the hell are you talking about, Jasmine?"

"Well, you work down there on certain shifts. I figured you could just . . . bring me one."

"Bring you one," Kendra echoed. "For what? To hold?"

Jasmine lowered her eyes. "To have," she whispered. The silence was deafening. Jasmine would've thought Kendra hadn't heard her if it wasn't for her quick intake of breath.

"Bitch, are you crazy? I can't believe you would ask me that." Kendra paused, waiting for a response, but Jasmine had none. "I'm going to chalk it up to the medicine talking," Kendra said. "And I know you're going through some things right now, so I'm going to pretend I didn't hear you ask me that. Get some rest. I'll check on you later."

Jasmine listened to the quiet click of the door shutting behind Kendra. She had figured her friend wouldn't go for it, and contrary to what Kendra surmised, it hadn't been the medicine talking. Or the heartbreak. She needed a baby. She needed Marcus. She needed that love. If she didn't have that, what was she living for?

Jasmine pulled the tape off the needle and slid it from her vein. A thin stream of blood gushed from the puncture. She stared at it for a moment, watching the blood stain the sheets. She held the pointy end of the needle to her wrist, welcoming the painful prick. She just needed to be quick. Just one swift stroke of the needle across her wrist and it would be over. All the pain. All the suffering.

She winced as she dragged the needle against her flesh and watched the blood spill from the gash. The monitor's incessant beeping increased, indicating the rise in her heart rate. She felt light headed. Just a little bit more—

Kendra burst into the room just then. "Jasmine, I forgot to ask if you wanted some food from—"

She gasped as Jasmine's hand froze. "Jasmine, what the fuck?"

She ran over and snatched the needle from Jasmine's hand. After grabbing a towel, Kendra pressed it to the wound. "What the hell is wrong with you?"

"I'm sorry." Jasmine's voice hitched as she cried. "I just don't want to live anymore, Kendra. I just don't—" Her breath caught in her throat, and she couldn't even finish the sentence. She felt dead inside.

Kendra pulled her into a hug and gently rubbed her back as Jasmine dissolved into muffled sobs. Her own tears wet Jasmine's hair. She swallowed. She knew what she had to do. "Okay," she whispered.

Jasmine looked up, searched her friend's eyes. Surely, she hadn't heard her. "What?"

"I said okay." Kendra took a staggered breath and shook her head in disbelief. She obviously couldn't believe the words, even as they fell from her lips. "I know a woman," she murmured. "In the maternity ward. She's been in there because she's having some complications. Keeps going into preterm labor. They're going to go ahead and induce her and put the baby in NICU. But she's a career woman. Says the pregnancy was an accident, and she already has a kid, so she's not sure if she wants another. She's asked me a few times if giving the baby up for adoption makes her a bad mother."

Jasmine's heart galloped in her chest, as she already envisioned the beautiful baby in her arms. It was perfect. "Okay, yes. Yes!" She was nearly screaming. "I want it. Please, Kendra. Please."

Kendra narrowed her eyes before relenting. "If I do this, Jasmine, you have to promise me you'll start going back to therapy. I can't stand to see you like this."

"Yes," Jasmine lied, her heart swelling with joy. *Fuck therapy.* She was going to get her baby, and she would have everything she wanted. Including Marcus.

Jasmine glanced in the rearview mirror for the tenth time and let out a relieved sigh when she saw the steady flow of cars passing by. No one seemed to notice her car parked at the curb or her body hunched down in the driver's seat as she watched the house. It looked like all the other houses on this block: an older Victorian-style abode with a wraparound porch and a detached two-car garage. It was the type of place where, at first sight, she would have never believed it belonged to her Marcus. But from following him home a few times before, she knew this was the little sanctuary he shared with his wife.

Jasmine still hadn't heard from him, and the lack of contact was making her crazy. So, she had had her car on two wheels as she sped to this side of town once she was released from the hospital. Now, three hours into her stakeout, she didn't know if she was happy or disappointed that she hadn't seen any type of activity.

It was getting dark. Kendra would be coming by her house soon, so Jasmine knew she needed to leave, but she was itching to go inside Marcus's house. She needed to know why the bastard hadn't returned her calls. Well, that was part of the reason. More than that, she just wanted to see what the big deal was about his wife and why he couldn't let her go. There was something oddly thrilling about the idea of snooping through Tracy's stuff, and she knew the bitch probably had a thing or two she could pawn.

With one last look in the rearview mirror, Jasmine stepped from the car and trotted across the street. She cut through a neighbor's yard and went around to the back of the house. The grass was thick with patches of dead leaves, which crunched under her sneakers. Stairs, weak from age, led up to a wooden deck that held a rusted barbecue grill and some patio furniture. Jasmine stood at the back door, and after glancing around once, she pulled her lockpick from her pocket. A couple of minutes later she had the knob turning and the door creaking open. Jasmine listened for an alarm, then grinned when she was met with silence.

The back door opened into a kitchen, updated with granite countertops and a slew of ivory cabinets, which took up three walls. Dirty dishes were stacked in the sink, and the smell of stale garbage had Jasmine covering her nose. She moseyed into the living room and noticed the framed wedding pictures collected on the coffee table. Jasmine smacked her teeth as she picked up one. For some reason, seeing her boyfriend all up in his wife's face brought on a fresh wave of anger, and she threw the picture to the floor. She smiled at the sound of the shattering glass and watching the shards fly across the floor. Damn, that felt good.

A surge of energy had Jasmine nearly running up the stairs. She needed to see their bedroom. Sure enough, the master suite was at the end of the hall. The bedroom was small, much smaller than hers, but their California king bed, which dominated the room, definitely made up for the lack of space. The plush red comforter was still pulled back, exposing wrinkled leopard sheets. It looked as if they had just gotten out of bed and left the house. A sick idea popped in her head, and Jasmine immediately stripped naked and left her clothes by the bedroom door.

She hopped in the bed. Being in the bed where Marcus slept with his wife was another erotic activity and immediately turned her on. Jasmine grabbed one of the pillows, one she hoped Tracy slept on, and rested it under her ass. She saw a framed picture of Marcus on the dresser, and focusing on that, Jasmine spread her legs and began using her fingers to massage her pussy. She pictured Marcus sucking on her clit while Tracy watched from the door, and Jasmine moaned, turned on by the image. She began fingering herself on the pillow, pumping her hips, and listened to the sloppy noises of her juices on her hand.

"Yes," she yelled in the empty room. She pictured Tracy's shocked expression, and she increased her finger-fucking speed. Imagining Marcus's lips lapping at her pretty folds until they were swollen and tingling, she came hard, releasing her juices all over the pillow, and her body quivered at the intensity of the orgasm.

When Jasmine was done, she used the sheet to wipe the sticky residue from her fingers, and she placed the pillow back in its place. Looking at the soaked-in stain on the pillowcase had her laughing hysterically. Oh, how she wished she could be there when Tracy came home and went to bed.

Jasmine went over to the dresser next. She wasn't looking for anything in particular in the dresser drawers, but she felt compelled to pull open each and every one and look inside. She came to a drawer with Marcus's boxers, and she pulled a pair out and put it to her face. She inhaled deeply and sighed as his scent filled her nostrils. Another drawer contained Tracy's clothes, and without thinking, Jasmine did the same thing. She covered her mouth and nose with a pair of panties and took a deep whiff of the cotton material. She shook her head as she replaced the garments. She had yet to see what the big deal was with this chick. Why did he even want her around? Tracy didn't have shit on her.

Jasmine moved to the closet. She knew this bitch was not nearly as fly as her, because nothing but cheap knockoffs hung on the racks. Not even bothering to think, Jasmine pulled all the clothes off the hangers, and after making a pile on the floor, she squatted over it and peed. Again, she knew what she had done was so absurd, but she couldn't help but laugh at herself. Marcus would be mad, but this escapade was definitely worth that ass whupping.

Jasmine put on her clothes and headed back downstairs. There was still no sign of Marcus or Tracy, and she had to keep ignoring the fact that wherever they were, they were probably together. But she knew not for too much longer. Kendra was on her way over to Jasmine's place, and she had promised to fulfill her request. So as far as

Jasmine was concerned, Tracy could kiss her ass and her precious husband goodbye.

Jasmine watched the clock and shifted anxiously on the sofa. It was almost nine, and she could barely contain her excitement.

It had taken some string pulling and hush money for some of the staff to look the other way, but everything was all set. Kendra would make some switches, but she would get a baby from the nursery, while making it look like the baby had died. The switch would be easy as long as Kendra hadn't grown some kind of conscience and ruined everything.

Jasmine rubbed the bandage around her wrist, struggling to relieve the itch. Each agonizing minute crawled by as her eyes toggled between the clock and the door. Where the hell was she? Just when she could feel the first prickles of anger, the doorbell rang. Jasmine flew from the sofa to answer the door. Sure enough, Kendra stood on the porch, still in her hospital scrubs, a carrier in her arms.

"Give her to me." Jasmine took the carrier and sat it on the living room floor. Her eyes hazed over with love as she eyed the sleeping baby nestled in the pink cushion. She was perfect. From her long eyelashes to the little brown ringlets that fell from underneath her baby cap. Her skin glowed and had an ombré appearance: the baby's honey complexion darkened to mahogany at her forehead and ears.

"Hi, precious," Jasmine cooed as she unhooked the restraints. The baby stirred. Jasmine gently lifted the tiny bundle and cradled her. "Thank you, Kendra. She is perfect."

Kendra remained quiet, watching the exchange. She struggled to ignore the guilt she felt. It had almost been traumatic delivering the news to the couple. This was their first little girl, and their hurt was very real. Especially when the young mother had requested to see the baby one last time to say goodbye. And Kendra had laid the dead baby in her arms. Jasmine's dead baby. And the woman had cried over the baby so much, it had pained Kendra to watch. Plus, she was scared. The father was a cop. What if he found out what had happened?

Jasmine remained oblivious to Kendra's stare as she carried the baby into the kitchen. "I bought milk," she said, her voice giddy with excitement. "Do you think she is hungry?"

"She's sleeping, Jasmine," Kendra said as she followed Jasmine into the kitchen.

"I know, but I wish she would wake up so I can play with her." Jasmine tapped the baby's cheek gently. "Come on, sweetie. Wake up for Mama."

"Jasmine, let her sleep." Kendra's voice was weary.

"Here. Do me a favor. Take her for a moment." She placed the baby in Kendra's arms without waiting for a response. "I need to call her daddy."

Jasmine picked up the phone and dialed Marcus for what had to be the hundredth time. He still had yet to return her calls or respond to any of her messages, but the baby's presence had joy over-riding her anger. "It's me, baby," she said on the voicemail. "Please call me back as soon as you get this. I want you to meet your daughter." Jasmine paused, eyeing the baby in Kendra's arms. "She looks just like you. Absolutely perfect. Please call me or come by. We want to see you. We love you." She held the phone out in the baby's direction. "Say hey to Daddy, sweetheart." She walked over and placed the device to the baby's ear. "Say hey, sweetie."

The baby turned her head, slightly fussy at the interruption of her sleep.

Kendra carried the baby back to her carrier. "Let her rest, Jasmine. Damn."

Jasmine clicked the phone off. She had done so much to be with him. She couldn't wait until he got the fuck out of his wife and came by so she could show him. She struggled to swallow the worry. It wasn't like Marcus to go this long without reaching out to her. Something was wrong. She prayed to God it wasn't serious.

She hated funerals.

Jasmine remained stoic as she eyed her reflection in the full-length mirror. The black empire-waist dress with a borderline risqué V-neck bodice and quarter sleeves was perfect for the occasion. A lace overlay took the dress from simple to romantically chic. She sighed. It would have to do.

The newspaper in which she had read and reread the article about Marcus's death until her head hurt was still on her vanity. A car accident. Neither he nor his wife had survived the single-car collision. She had struggled not to slip into another bout of depression. He had never even made it to see their daughter.

As if on cue, Gabrielle began making fussy noises in her crib. Jasmine eyed the baby. She and Marcus were supposed to have that fairy-tale marriage and raise their baby together like a real family. So, she had done what she needed to do to make that happen. But what had that gotten her? Stuck as a single mother. She hadn't wanted the baby so much as she had wanted Marcus. Now what was she going to do with her?

Gabrielle's whimpers turned into full-fledged cries, and she hollered at the top of her tiny lungs until she broke out in a sweat. Jasmine tuned out the noise as she continued to curl her hair until the sixteen inches fell in huge coils that framed her face. The doorbell rang right on time, and Jasmine went down the steps to answer the door.

When she opened the front door, she found Kendra standing on the porch, shaking the rain from her umbrella. Kendra immediately frowned when she heard the baby's distant sobs. "Jazz, damn, do you want the baby to cry herself sick?" Kendra dropped the umbrella on the porch and led the way upstairs.

Jasmine went straight to the dresser to start applying her makeup. She listened to Kendra coo at the baby until her cries diminished to soft whimpers once more.

"No wonder she is pissed. You need to change her, Jasmine."

"Her auntie Kenny is here now. I need to get ready for this funeral."

Kendra shook her head at her friend's apathy. She lifted the baby in her arms. The swollen Pampers diaper had soiled the edges of her onesie and bits of doo-doo had crusted on her thighs. "You're the one that wanted this baby." She muttered her disapproval.

Jasmine would've rolled her eyes if she hadn't been applying eyeliner. "Don't start," she said.

"I'm just saying you didn't see how her mother was—"

"So?" Jasmine snapped as she turned to face her friend. "I don't care. I just lost my boyfriend, Kendra. I don't want to hear this shit right now. I'm dealing with a lot." She turned back to the mirror; her reddened eyes focused on her makeup again. "I'm Gabby's mother now."

Kendra remained quiet as she gently patted the baby's back. Her friend's anguish was eating at her. She wanted to ask if Jasmine had started seeing the therapist, like she had promised, but she already knew the answer. Jasmine was on what appeared to be a downward spiral, and by the looks of it, she did not care to dig herself out.

"We'll be here when you get back," Kendra said curtly before carrying the baby out of the room.

Jasmine didn't respond. Her mind was on the fact that this was about to be one awkward-ass funeral.

The walkway outside the church was thick with mourners. A light rain fell, and people stood in clusters under umbrellas, speaking in hushed tones and dabbing at their cheeks with damp tissues. Then they filed solemnly into the church.

Jasmine felt eyes on her as she slid into one of the back pews. Two coffins rested at the front, angled diagonally from the altar, and a framed picture of each of the deceased stood on top of the powder-blue stainless steel. Just looking at the headshot of Marcus, that sexy smile, those eyes exuding warmth, brought more tears to her eyes.

Once everyone was seated, the pastor stood at the front, adorned with a cream and purple robe. He signaled to the musicians to silence the music. "Good afternoon." His greeting was met with a few solemn murmurs. "We are here today to seek and receive comfort. Not one, but two souls have been called home to be with the Lord, and though our hearts ache, we must find peace by trusting and relying heavily on God. Not just in this time of need, but always. Proverbs chapter three, verse five says, 'Trust in the Lord with all thine heart and lean not unto thine own understanding.' We are going to move past the tears, the questions, and the doubt. For God does not make mistakes. And the Holy Spirit is here today to comfort and strengthen each of our hearts. And He will continue to be with us as we continue to live for God."

The pastor quoted a few more scriptures; then someone belted a tear-jerking rendition of Yolanda Adams's "I'm Gonna Be Ready."

Sight beyond what I see
You know what's best for me
Prepare my mind, prepare my heart
For whatever comes, I'm gonna be ready. . . .

Even after the woman hit the last note, the musicians continued to play. Jasmine sagged in the pew, her body weak from grief.

"Now," the pastor said, continuing with the ceremony, "we'll have a few words from Marcus's father."

Jasmine shut her eyes and listened to the older man climb the steps. Then his familiar voice cracked as he spoke into the podium microphone. It took every ounce of energy for her to lift her head and watch him utter each painful word of the eulogy. As much as her heart ached from losing the love of her life, she knew that ache was even worse for Grant Weston, as he had lost his only child.

By the time the mourners had migrated to the cemetery, the rain had slacked off to a gentle mist. The gray clouds above definitely underscored the gloomy mood of the entire service. Jasmine kept her distance as she observed both caskets being lowered side by side into the moist soil of the adjacent burial plots. Grant and his wife sat on the fold-out chairs closest to the plots. She couldn't help but notice his bitch Sheila was dressed like she was straight out of Hollywood, complete with a black birdcage veil and satin gloves that spanned the length of her arms. Jasmine rolled her eyes. She had never been able to stand Sheila. Had never met the chick personally, but as Grant's sugar baby, she couldn't help the periodic twinges of jealousy over how he pampered her up in some mansion, letting her prance around and flossing her for the cameras while she had to stay "Daddy's little secret."

Jasmine continued to survey the guests. The media had been all over the story because of Grant's notoriety, but the family had insisted on a closed service. Surprise etched her face when she suddenly noticed Patricia in the crowd. What the hell was she doing her? Then Jasmine spotted someone else, despite the huge sunglasses, the brown braid wig. She was sitting in the driver's seat of a car parked in a parking lot a substantial distance away, but Jasmine knew it was Jayla.

The gasp escaped her lips even before her mind had time to register fully Jayla's presence. Jasmine didn't even attempt to hide the fact that she was staring. All the memories of the past year came barreling back in a wave of disgust and anger. *So that's what Patricia is doing at the funeral. That's what she was doing at my doctor's appointment*, she thought. *Stalking me to report back to Jayla*. Jasmine scanned the crowd for Patricia again. When she looked back over at the parking lot, she frowned when she saw the empty space where Jayla's car had just been. She blinked, almost unsure if she had even seen the car at all.

Minutes later the burial service concluded, and the crowd began to disperse. Jasmine immediately headed toward Patricia. She couldn't even focus on her grief right now. All this shady, conniving shit was pissing her off. She caught up with Patricia as she was making her way across the cemetery, her long black dress almost baggy on her tiny frame.

"Hey!"

Patricia turned and gave her a weak smile. "Jasmine. What are—" Her sentence was cut off by Jasmine's slap on her cheek.

"You want to stalk me so you can run your mouth to Jayla. You and that bitch better stay away from me, or I swear, your asses are as good as dead." She turned and stalked off, leaving Patricia smirking, despite the red mark on her face.

CHAPTER NINE

Jayla

What the fuck was she doing there? Jayla wondered as she floored the gas pedal and swerved to narrowly pass an eighteen-wheeler. Her mind was reeling with angry confusion as images of her airport arrest clouded her vision. Jasmine had been so smug on the phone. So damn triumphant. And she had had that entitled attitude, like a peasant who had dethroned the queen. She had some fucking nerve.

Jayla marinated on Jasmine's presence at the funeral so long, she felt the beginnings of a headache. Something definitely was going on, and she would need to get to the bottom of it. Especially because she didn't trust Jasmine. The bitch was backstabbing, conniving, and vindictive. The fact that she was somehow involved made Jayla nervous, because she knew the girl was up to some shit.

Jayla sighed as her thoughts turned to the funeral. Fear had prompted her to make the murder request to Sheila. She had still been traumatized by her near-death experience at the hands of Marcus and his psychotic sister-in-law/girlfriend, Lauren. Yes, Lauren had died, but Marcus had somehow survived the ordeal. Killing him had been the only option. It was survival of the fittest. Kill or be killed. And she had made sure her trigger was pulled first. Never in a million years had she thought he was Grant's son.

The incident had gotten a lot of press, but the media had written it off as an accident for now, as evidenced by the headline in a local paper two days later: SENATOR'S SON AND WIFE KILLED IN CAR ACCIDENT. This was good for her in the short term, but she was sure that the cops would find evidence of foul play soon enough. She hadn't necessarily planned Tracy's death, but maybe it was for the better. She didn't want to worry about some bitch coming after her on some revenge-type vendetta.

But why had Sheila gone along with the plan? What kind of crazy woman was okay with having her son killed? And what the hell was Jasmine doing at the funeral? What was her involvement? There were just too many moving pieces. Too many questions. And she needed answers.

Jayla wheeled the car into a nearby shopping center, parked, and pulled out her phone. She didn't even bother with a text, just dialed the number and placed the phone to her ear.

"Yes, ma'am?" Sheila answered too quickly, as if she was expecting the call.

"Sheila, we need to talk."

Silence. Finally, she asked, "Where are you?"

"Farmer's Market on Ponce."

"On my way." There was the click of the call ending.

Jayla pulled off her wig, pulled her hair back from her face, and used a rubber band in her cup holder to fasten it into a ponytail. She settled in the seat and waited.

An hour later, a crisp white Benz eased into the parking space next to hers. Jayla watched as Sheila emerged from the car. She had changed into some white leggings and a sea-blue blouse, and she wore a set of owl-size gold sunglasses, which shielded half of her face. No one could tell she had just come from a funeral.

As if Jayla didn't see her, Sheila stooped down next to the passenger window and tapped her finger on the class.

Jayla rolled down the window. "Get in."

"No, you get out," Sheila countered with a smirk. "Let's get something to eat."

"I'm not hungry."

"I am."

Frustrated, Jayla rolled her eyes, shut off the engine, and climbed out from behind the wheel. This bitch was clearly into games.

They strolled down the pavilion sidewalk in silence before Sheila finally spoke first. “Go ahead. What did you want to talk about?”

Jayla scoffed. “What did I want to talk about? For starters, why the hell didn’t you tell me Marcus was your son?”

As was her custom, Sheila reached in her pocket for a cigarette. “First off, don’t get it twisted. He was my stepson.” The simple statement was tossed out like a justification. As if it made it better.

Jayla was stunned. Surely, Sheila was on some other type of lunacy. “Son, stepson . . . What the fuck does it matter? How could you?”

“What? Kill him? Isn’t that what you wanted me to handle for you? I asked you if you were sure.”

“Yeah, but that was because he was going to come after me,” Jayla snapped. “I don’t make a point of doing shit like that for thrills. Him and his little loony tune side piece held me hostage and tried to kill me. Hell, I was scared. But I didn’t know he was your damn son.”

“*Stepson*,” Sheila said, correcting her, before taking a deep drag from her cigarette. “Look. You asked me to get rid of him for you. I did. Did I know who he was when you first told me?” She shrugged. “Maybe a part of me did. Did I care?

Hell no. I never liked that greedy bastard in the first place. And the way I see it, that means more money back in Grant's wallet." Sheila stopped speaking and faced Jayla, then gently rubbed her knuckles down Jayla's cheek and went even farther to graze her breast. "We have an arrangement. That's what I care about."

Jayla could only look on in disgust at this woman's insensitivity. Hell, even she was feeling guilty after finding out Marcus was Grant's son. She searched Sheila's eyes for some shred of remorse. But she saw none. Sheila gazed back at her with lust-filled eyes as she puffed lazily on that damn cigarette. She was the epitome of a coldhearted bitch.

"So. Any more questions?"

Jayla suddenly remembered something. "Yeah. Why was Jasmine at the funeral?"

"Who?"

"Jasmine. Young girl. About twenty or so. Layered brown hair."

Sheila shrugged. "I don't know who you're talking about."

Jayla was sure her facial expression conveyed the doubt she felt. Sheila was lying. She just knew it. The question was, why?

"I have to go," Sheila said, flicking her cigarette to the ground and crushing it under her shoe. "You enjoy the rest of your day." Sheila tapped her finger on her watch to let Jayla know time was still ticking. She then crossed the parking lot and headed back toward her car.

Jayla wondered if Sheila realized she never did get anything to eat, since she was oh so hungry. She smacked her lips. Yeah, she didn't trust that bitch any further than she could see her. And that was dangerous, given the new assignment, and now the murder on her hands. Things were getting heavy.

Jayla had turned to head back to her car when she spotted him. Damn, the sight of him still had her heart fluttering and her kitty moistening her satin panties. He hadn't changed a bit. His head was still clean shaven, showing every piece of his smooth chocolate skin. He had a stubble of a goatee, which now rimmed his lips. He was flashing that million-dollar smile, his dimples even more evident, as he engaged in a phone conversation. She wanted to melt right there.

Before she knew it, her feet were moving in his direction. She hadn't seen Derrick in forever. And there he was, sitting casually on an outside bench, as if he were waiting for her. She remembered how just a year or so ago, she was engaged to him, was planning her wedding, and they were preparing to start their lives together. Her heart ached with the love she still had for him. This man, this piece of herself, she was ready to give it all up for him. But then she remembered that conversation with his mother, Gloria. *Do you deserve my son?* The lie had come easily then, but now it was so painfully obvious. No. No, she didn't deserve him. She was tainted goods. He did deserve better, but she was willing to be better if it meant she could still have him.

Jayla was so close now, she could almost taste him, and her mouth watered. She took a deep breath, inhaling the familiar cinnamon and citrus scent he always carried with him. Damn, he even smelled the same. "Derrick," she whispered.

Derrick looked up, and the smile fell from his lips as he stared at her, expressionless. "Hey, let me call you back," he said into the phone before clicking it off to disconnect the call.

He rose, and Jayla turned her head to meet his eyes as he stood in front of her. He had apparently been working out too. His shoulders were a little broader. There now seemed to be more definition in the ripple of muscle under his sleeves. For a while, he just stared, and Jayla held her breath. The suspense was killing her. Once upon a time, she could all but read his thoughts. They had been so in sync. As bad as she had hurt him, now she was sure he hated her. The painful possibility had tears spilling down her cheeks.

"I'm sorry," she murmured, breaking the silence.

"Wow, Jayla." Derrick sighed. "I wondered what I would say if I saw you again. Damn, I'm speechless."

Jayla forced a smile. "I still have that effect on you, huh?" The weak attempt at humor only heightened the strained tension. She cleared her throat. "Can we go somewhere and talk?"

"We really don't have anything to talk about."

"Please? I just need to talk to you. I never got a chance to explain."

Derrick narrowed his eyes, and Jayla felt as if she were being dissected with a knife and fork. What was he thinking? Why was he watching her like that? He looked to the sky, and there she saw it. The devastation. The anguish. He wanted to be angry, but she had absolutely destroyed him with her selfish actions. Jayla choked, struggling to hold in her need to crumple to the pavement and sob at his feet.

"I was so angry with you," he said through gritted teeth. "The anger consumed me. It ate at me. Day and night. I wondered what I had done to deserve that pain and suffering—"

"It wasn't your fault, Derrick," Jayla said, cutting him off, desperate to explain. "It was me. All me. I was stupid and selfish, and I tried to have my cake and eat it too. You didn't deserve that. If you could just let me explain, I'm willing to do whatever it takes to make you happy. To remind you why you fell in love with me. I'm still that same woman."

When he didn't respond, Jayla chanced stepping forward and placing her hand on his arm. "Derrick," she said, somehow feeling a sense of hope. There had to be something still there for them. They had been so in love. "Please tell me it's not too late for us. Please tell me there is still a chance. I love you."

Derrick's eyes fell to her hand on him. He let out a breath. "Remember when I saw you dropping that ring off and I tried to call you that day?"

Jayla nodded. Of course she remembered. In the airport she had rejected the incoming call because she was attempting to start over, and she had realized he was better off without her. If only she could go back to that moment.

"I thought that there was still a chance. I thought I could get past everything, because I loved you to my core. You just don't know." He paused. "But then I got a call."

"Huh?"

Derrick's eyes lifted to hers again. "HIV, Jayla?"

Jayla felt the life drain from her. *Please, God, no.* "Derrick. You don't have it, do you?" His silence answered the question, and she felt the shock snatch her breath. Her chest tightened, and she couldn't help crying, the hot tears stinging her cheeks and blurring her vision. There had been only a few times in her life when she wished she could die. Now was one of them.

"It's taken a lot of therapy and prayer, Jayla," Derrick said. He made no move to comfort her. "And I forgive you. I do. But there is no way in hell there could ever be anything between us again."

Jayla nodded. Shame colored her face, but she couldn't say she was actually surprised by his response. She had tried and failed, but it was her own damn fault.

"Sorry about that, sweetie. He made a real stinky this time."

The familiar voice had Jayla's face creasing in a frown. *Sweetie?* She looked up, and her eyes widened from shock as Tara, her ex-best friend, approached them, a curly-haired baby boy strapped in the baby travel carrier she wore across her chest.

"Jayla?" Now it was Tara's turn to frown, and her eyes flared from renewed rage. "What the fuck are you doing here?"

"Baby, calm down." Derrick took a step between them and rested his hands on Tara's shoulders.

The protective gesture infuriated Jayla, for some reason. "What the hell is going on here?" she said.

"Bitch, you got some nerve to be rolling up on my man and asking us about our business," Tara snapped back.

The statement was enough to knock the wind out of Jayla. *Man?*

"Take DJ to the car, baby," Derrick said. "Now. I'm coming."

Tara cut her eyes at Jayla one last time before turning and stalking off. She stopped suddenly, turned, and called back, "Oh, and, Jayla, it was your slut behavior that brought me and Derrick together. So, I guess I should be thanking you for bringing me my true soul mate and father to my son." With the last comment, Tara lifted her hand in the air to show the engagement ring winking on her finger.

CHAPTER TEN

Jasmine

Jasmine bucked on his face, massaging his tongue with her clit until it was throbbing.

Grant gripped her ass as she rode. He moaned, urging her to keep up the momentum as he sucked on her kitty like it was honeysuckle. The subtle vibration sent a ripple through her sensitive flesh.

"Yes," she gasped, bracing against the headboard. She released, allowing her juices to flow free, and he slurped and swallowed her nectar, polishing every crease of her plump lips.

Spent, Jasmine climbed down from her position on his face and leaned over to taste her own fluids on his tongue. She felt Grant's lips turn up into a smile. "Thank you," she murmured against his mouth. "I needed that."

Grant remained quiet as she slid beneath the sheets and wrapped her arms around his chest. She knew his mind was on Marcus. Hers had been too. She fantasized it was Marcus she was with every time they sexed. But they had been interacting differently since his death.

As soon as she got comfortable, Grant pulled away and climbed out of the bed. Jasmine sat up, confused. It was strange for him to not want to fuck. Or at least get some head or booty action. But she remained quiet as he began dressing. Her eyes slid to the clock. Maybe it was for the better if he hurried and left. Kendra was due back from the park with Gabrielle pretty soon. And Grant really didn't need to be here when they returned.

"Mister, you know what I was thinking?" Jasmine kissed Grant's shoulder when he sat on the bed to put on his socks. "That we should get away, baby. Just you and me. Naked and fucking on some white sandy beach. How does that sound?"

Grant sighed. "Baby girl, you know I can't get away right now. I've got a lot of press events to do because of Marcus's death."

"Oh," Jasmine replied, exaggerating the note of disappointment in her voice. She honestly knew he wouldn't be able to go, and she didn't give a damn. She was the one that needed the vacation. "Well, do you think I could go and you could just meet me, if you can, when things calm down?"

"That's fine." Grant glanced at his watch and leaned in to kiss Jasmine on the forehead. "Just give me the details, and I'll make it happen. Oh. I almost forgot." He reached into his jacket pocket and pulled out a velvet box. "I meant to give you this a while back, but with everything . . . It's just a little something to show you how much you mean to me."

Jasmine grinned as she accepted the box and popped it open. Her eyes twinkled at the diamond-encrusted gold tennis bracelet. The delicate stones caught the light and sent rays glittering across the sheets. Giddy, she threw her arms around his neck and kissed him. "Thank you, baby."

"My pleasure. You know I love doing things for you. You actually appreciate me."

"Of course." Jasmine looked into his eyes, feigning sincerity. "You know I care for you very much. It hurts me to see you're hurting about your son. That's why I want us to go away together. I love you too much to see you suffering."

"Thank you, baby girl." Grant plucked the bracelet from the box and clipped it on around her wrist. "So, do you like it?"

"I love it. You know me so well."

Grant chuckled. "I actually can't take credit for this. I was clueless. I met a nice woman in the store who picked it out."

"Well, she has excellent taste in jewelry." Jasmine crawled forward on her knees, then nuzzled Grant's neck as she lowered her voice seductively and asked, "Do I need to be jealous, Mister?"

"Of course not." He turned to kiss her.

Just then the doorbell rang, startling them both. Jasmine scrambled from the bed and snatched her satin robe from the floor. *Shit.* Kendra was back.

"Who is that?" Grant walked to the window and peeped through the blinds. "I told you before I don't really like you having company."

Jasmine combed her fingers through her hair as she headed for the steps. "I know, sweetie. It's just my sister and my niece. Just wait right here and let me get rid of them." She cursed herself as she nearly ran to the front door. She should've told Kendra she would come pick up Gabrielle, but Grant's visit had been last minute.

"Here you go, ma'am." Kendra held out the carrier as soon as Jasmine pulled open the door. "I think she needs changing. You should've heard her going at it in the car. Pooping and stinking up my seats."

Jasmine eyed Gabrielle, who was amusing herself by blowing spit bubbles and giggling at the noise. She continued to block the front door. "Can you come back in a little bit?" she whispered.

Kendra frowned. "Uh, no, I cannot. You told me to give you a few hours, because you were sick, and I did. Now here." She shoved the carrier in Jasmine's arms. "Take your daughter, because I have to go to work."

"Kendra. Just give me a minute. Can you just wait in the car with her or something?"

"Why? You have company?" Kendra glanced toward the black Benz she had parked behind in the driveway. She crossed her arms over her breasts.

Jasmine's flimsy robe, her disheveled hair . . . It was more than obvious why she had insisted on an emergency babysitter.

Catching her off guard, Kendra pushed past Jasmine and stormed into the foyer. She glanced around the empty space. "So where is he, huh?" she yelled. "You in here fucking some dude, Jasmine, really? What about your boyfriend, who you were boo-hooing and crying about at the funeral the other week? How you gone play me?"

Jasmine's eyes darted to the stairs, and frantic, she muttered, "Sh!" in a weak attempt to quiet her friend's rant.

"Bitch, don't shush me," Kendra snapped. "You pretend like you're so sick, so I offer to take *your* daughter to the park so you can get some rest. Next thing I know, I come back, and your lying ass just finished having sex. What the hell, Jasmine?"

"Can you keep your damn voice down?" Jasmine hissed. She hoped Grant wasn't hearing any of this. "Look, just leave the damn baby and get the hell out of my house."

"No! I want to know who is so important that you keep pushing Gabrielle off on me," Kendra said. "Is it your sugar daddy? Your precious Mister? The one who bought you this house and gives you all this damn money just for you throwing some pussy in his face?"

Jasmine was furious. Who was this chick to judge her like her shit didn't stink? Kendra was mad because Jasmine had a sugar daddy who gave her whatever the hell she wanted just for showing him a little attention. "Bitch, what the fuck is wrong with you? Why you hatin'?" The baby started wailing, but neither woman seemed to notice.

"Hatin'?"

"Yeah. You're jealous. I'm sorry that I have a man that loves me and wants to be with me, and I have all the material shit you do times ten. And I ain't got to work seventy hours a damn week for it."

Kendra narrowed her eyes. If it wasn't for the baby carrier Jasmine was holding, she would've served this arrogant bitch a lethal ass whupping. "So, taking this baby? It was all for nothing, right?"

Jasmine's face paled, and her eyes darted back to the stairs. She thought she saw a shadow at the top of the landing, but she couldn't be sure. "I don't know what you're talking about. Get out of my house, before I call the police," she yelled, fear sharpening her tone of voice.

The baby was still crying, and her precious face had turned pink as she screamed to anyone who would hear.

"You don't even act like her mother. You don't do shit for her. I do. What the hell are you trying to prove?"

"I ain't trying to prove shit," Jasmine snapped. "I love this child. Now, get the fuck out now!"

Kendra shook her head and dropped the diaper bag on the floor. The baby's crying pulled at her heartstrings, and she wished to God she hadn't taken her from her biological parents. She figured poor Gabrielle would've been better off with them than she was with Jasmine, who had apparently lost touch with reality.

"This is probably why your baby died in the first damn place," she hissed, not caring as the hurtful words dripped from her lips. "Because God knew your stupid ass didn't need no damn child. I'm out."

Kendra rushed across the foyer, pulled open the front door, and ran smack into two police officers standing on the porch. She froze, praying to God they weren't looking for her. The baby snatching from the hospital was sure to put her in the jail.

The white cop flashed his badge. "Jasmine Morgan?"

Kendra shook her head and gestured behind her at the woman in the foyer.

Jasmine approached the front door. Her eyes ballooned when she spotted the police. "Um, can I help you?"

"Jasmine Morgan?" said the white cop.

Jasmine shook her head. "Yes?"

The cop grabbed Jasmine's arm. "Jasmine Morgan, you're under arrest."

"For what?"

"For the murder of Tracy and Marcus Weston."

Jasmine's blood ran cold as she felt the handcuffs being snapped on her wrists. This couldn't be happening. She struggled, and her robe fell open, exposing her naked body. But neither she nor the cops seemed to notice, as they held on to her while reading her, her rights and she kept flailing her arms.

"This is a mistake," she yelled. "Please. Kendra, tell them!"

Shock had Kendra planted to the porch, and she shook her head, struggling to make sense of the allegation.

Jasmine didn't care that she was resisting arrest. She kicked and bucked until the cops finally had to slam her to the porch floorboards. The white officer's knee jabbed her right between the shoulder blades, and she yelped in pain. She must have hit her head in the tussle, because her vision was beginning to blur. But not before she looked through the open front door and caught a glimpse of Grant on the stairs, his face crinkled in what looked to be a menacing frown at everything he had heard.

Destroy or be destroyed. There is only room for one. Strategy Part 2: Conquer. I'll be the last one standing when all is said and done. . . .

CHAPTER ELEVEN

Jayla

Jayla had been crying and nursing a bottle of Cîroc, so she didn't even hear Patricia padding into the kitchen.

"Puma?" Patricia flicked on the overhead light with a frown, and Jayla winced at the sudden glare. "What are you doing in here? It's two in the morning."

Jayla shrugged, grabbed the bottle by the neck, and downed another mouthful. The alcohol stung her throat, but she welcomed the burn.

Sighing, Patricia wrapped her robe around herself a little tighter and moved to the stool beside Jayla's. She watched the tears streaking down Jayla's cheeks, but instead of questioning her again, she waited.

"I thought me getting out was a good thing," Jayla began after taking a few more sips of her drink. "The whole time I was locked up, I couldn't wait to get out, because I thought I had some piece of a life left. Everything just keeps getting worse and worse."

"What happened?"

"I saw Derrick today." Jayla shut her eyes at the painful revelation. If only she could forget. If only it wasn't real, and her eyes had been playing tricks on her. "He's with Tara now. They're engaged."

"So, you saw them, huh?"

The unexpected response had Jayla's head whipping up in confusion. "You knew, Patricia? You knew, and you didn't tell me?"

"I still talk to Derrick's mom, Gloria, from time to time," Patricia admitted. "She mentioned something like that."

Desperate to unleash her temper, Jayla turned on her. "What the hell, Patricia? You knew, and you didn't tell me!"

Patricia remained calm at the outburst. "And why would I do that, Puma? So, you can sit up here, knocking back liquor for breakfast? Look at you. I didn't want to see you like this. I knew it would hurt you, because he meant so much to you."

Means to me, Jayla thought, correcting the tense, with a staggering sigh. Her heart was hurting like hell. "I still love him," she said out loud. To her surprise, Patricia chuckled. She frowned, then was silently satisfied when the woman's chuckle turned into a collection of coughs. Served her ass right, because wasn't shit funny about this situation.

"Let me educate you," Patricia said after her coughing fit was over. "Again. That love shit is for the birds. I told you when I got you started, you could hang up that Disney happily ever after. So what? You were thinking you could come out and still marry Derrick and he was gone forget all the shit you've done?"

The bite of truth had Jayla rolling her eyes and taking another swig of the Cîroc. "I keep forgetting how you can be a coldhearted bitch sometimes," she grumbled.

Patricia chuckled at the insult. "Damn right," she smirked. "I keep it one hundred, so if you expect fifty, read *Fifty Shades of Grey*."

"What the hell are they even doing together?" Jayla asked more herself than Patricia. "That is foul. My best friend, though?"

"Puma, you make it sound like something on Jerry Springer. You're not with him, and you're not even friends with her anymore."

"It doesn't make it any better." Jayla blew out a frustrated breath. "How did that even happen?"

"Gloria said Tara left her husband," Patricia revealed. "Mind you, she was pregnant, but she divorced that man really quick after she found out he had slept with you."

"He blackmailed me," Jayla whined, squeezing her eyes shut against the truth. "He knew I was an appraiser and threatened to tell Derrick if I didn't sleep with him. I didn't want to do it."

"I know, but still, you know your friend wasn't trying to hear that." Patricia's small smile was one of pity. "Anyway, Tara left, and she took everything. And I mean everything. Didn't leave him with a pot to piss in or a pair of drawers to catch the drips. So, she and Derrick were both upset after finding out everything with you and started comforting each other or something. He was pretty much there during her whole pregnancy, so when she had him, Gloria said they named the baby DJ or Derrick Jr. or something."

"So now they're all in love?" Jealous bitterness had the words feeling like acid on her tongue. Jayla didn't give a damn what she had done. That shit was fucked up from every angle. The pain was sitting on her chest like a brick, but she was beginning to feel the anger eclipse her hurt.

Jayla wondered if Gloria had relayed the news about Derrick's HIV and the fact that she, Jayla, was the one who had given it to him. The news was tearing her up inside, and that was the real reason she knew she now meant nothing to Derrick. And she loved him too much. To know she had never been any good for him, not even at the moment they met, was enough to make her sick. But part of her also wondered about Tara and whether she had HIV. And the baby.

Jayla opened her mouth to reveal the truth when Patricia spoke first. "Such is life, Puma," she said, with a deflated sigh. "We're all dealt a shitty hand. Me included."

Jayla held her breath. Did she already know? "What do you mean?" she asked. It was then she noticed Patricia's red-rimmed eyes, glossed over with tears.

Patricia took her time standing, leaning on the counter for support. She made her way to the bay window, and Jayla could see her sad face in the reflection in the glass.

"I have lymphocytic leukemia," she said, hugging herself to stop trembling. "Bone cancer. I've known about it for some time now."

Jayla's heart raced as she waited for a sign that this confession was a joke. It couldn't be true. There was no way she could've been so wrapped up in her own twisted life that the woman she loved, the woman she looked up to, was dying right in front of her. When Patricia sank to the hardwood floor, Jayla's heart shattered. She ran to Patricia's side, knelt down, and hugged her.

"I don't believe it." Jayla was all but sobbing into the synthetic tresses of Patricia's wig. "There has to be something. Chemo. Something. You can survive this. People do it all the time."

Patricia gave a watery smile and gingerly pulled the wig off.

Jayla shook her head, as if denying the image before her of her mentor's bald scalp. "No," she said desperately. "Patricia, fight this. It's not too late."

"Puma, I'm tired. I've done everything I can, and I'm done. I've accepted this," she croaked. "I need you to accept it too."

Jayla rested her cheek against Patricia's, allowing their tears to merge. "How long?"

"Not long." Patricia's words were heavy. "So, I want you to finish this last job with Sheila and be done with this shit. Be finally done with this once and for all."

They lay there, hugging each other, and eventually dozed off. When the first rays of sun spilled through the window, Jayla stirred. She lay still, listening to Patricia's congested snore, and she gently kissed the woman's forehead. Patricia was right. She needed to finish this assignment, and just maybe there was some life for her outside this sex business. Jayla then remembered she hadn't told Patricia about the HIV, after all. But at this point, with the woman's body riddled with cancer as she lay sleeping in her arms, it didn't even seem to matter.

Jayla shifted the gift basket to her other arm as she rode the elevator up to Grant's office. She knew she looked delicious in her all-black skinny-leg jumper and black lace wig. Makeup was minimal, as was customary for her, but she had made sure to brush on her fire-red gloss, which had her lips looking big and bold. Her gold Coach heels clicked on the hardwood as she stepped off the elevator and headed to the front desk.

The receptionist eyed her suspiciously over the thin frames of her glasses. She frowned. “May I help you?”

“Yes. I need to see Senator Weston.”

The woman’s eyes dropped to her computer screen. “I don’t see an appointment on the schedule.”

“Oh, excuse me . . .” Jayla eyed the gold nameplate resting on the desk. “Barbara. You didn’t even ask me my name to see if I have an appointment.”

Barbara glanced back up and eyed Jayla’s revealing attire, her forehead creased in disdain. “Senator Weston’s next appointment is with Congressman Phillips, and then he has a press conference. I seriously doubt you are Congressman Phillips, since he is an older Caucasian gentleman with a wife and three children.”

Jayla rolled her eyes from irritation. “Can you please let him know I’m here?” she snapped. “I am a friend, and I’ve stopped by to bring this to him.” Jayla lifted the basket onto the glass desk. “The man just lost his son. It’s not all about business all the time.”

Barbara’s eyes softened a fraction, but it was clear she was still conflicted over what she should do about this visitor. "Senator Weston doesn't see walk-ins—"

"How about you tell him I'm here and we let *him* decide if he wants to see me?"

The receptionist sighed, obviously just as frustrated as Jayla. "Please have a seat, and I'll call him for you."

"If you don't mind, I'll wait right here while you call," Jayla said with a plastic smile.

"Fine." Barbara's tone was clipped when she lifted the phone and said, "Who shall I say is visiting?"

"Rochelle, from the jewelry store," Jayla said, and the woman's face wrinkled from confusion. "He'll know who I am," she added. "I helped him pick out a bracelet for his daughter."

"Mr. Weston doesn't have—" The sound of a collection of male voices had Barbara stopping in mid-sentence. They both looked down the hallway just as a group of men rounded the corner.

"I'll speak at the school board meeting next week," Grant was saying. "The administrators should know about the fund allocations for the upcoming school year."

Carl, the same man who had accompanied Grant to the jewelry store, was in tow. Guard or assistant or both, Jayla still didn't know his function. There were also four other men, whom she guessed were congressional officials and staffers.

"Thank you so much for meeting with us, Senator," one man said as he shook Grant's hand.

"My pleasure." After an exchange of professional handshakes, the congressional folks dispersed, and Grant and Carl remained in the hallway, chatting about some paperwork.

Jayla seized the window of opportunity before the receptionist had a chance to open her mouth. "Senator Weston," she called. She watched Grant turn, and then his eyes roamed over her body before settling on her face. Judging by his curious stare, she knew he couldn't place her. "Rochelle," Jayla reminded him and flashed a smile. "From the jewelry store. I helped you pick out the—"

"The tennis bracelet," Grant interrupted with a nod. "Yes, of course. How may I help you?"

Jayla lifted the gift basket into view. "I was in the area, and I wanted to bring this by. Do you have a moment? I won't be long."

"Sir, I informed Ms. Rochelle that you have a meeting," Barbara announced, quickly jumped into the conversation.

"I have time," Grant said. He handed a stack of folders to the man beside him. "Carl, take these to the conference room for me. I'll be there shortly." Grant gestured for Jayla to follow him.

Jayla tossed a sly grin to the receptionist and, lowering her voice so only she could hear, said, "That's for trying to cock block. You answer phones.

Get your life together and stop taking your job so damn seriously all the time." With that, Jayla strutted down the hall after Grant Weston.

Grant opened the door to his office to reveal a huge executive desk, a woven fleece rug in vibrant hues of red, and framed certificates in a strategic cluttered arrangement on the wall above the fireplace. He closed the door behind her, and Jayla had to commend herself on her choice of attire when she felt her body tingling from his gaze.

Jayla turned and handed him the basket. "For you," she said. "I wanted to come by and express my condolences for the loss of your son."

Grant's eyes clouded with grief as he took the gift. "Thank you. This is very thoughtful of you." He moved to sit the basket on his desk. "It's been very difficult. I've just been burying myself in my work to escape it."

"That's not healthy. But I know people cope with grief in different ways." Jayla remembered her own sister Jocelyn, who everyone thought had committed suicide but who had really been murdered by Lauren and Marcus. She pinched her eyes shut. The pain of death was still just as fresh as a new sore, and she let out a staggered breath. Jocelyn, Aunt Bev, her mother. And soon, perhaps, Patricia. Her mind wandered to their conversation. She didn't know what she would do if she lost Patricia too.

When Jayla opened her eyes, she saw Grant had moved over to the fireplace and was eyeing something on the mantel. She briefly looked at the picture he was staring at before snatching her eyes away. She didn't need any visual reminders of Marcus. After what he had done, he had deserved to die, and she had no regrets for having him killed.

"You should get away for a while," she suggested. "Sometimes a change of scenery helps."

Grant chuckled. "So I've heard." He turned to look at Jayla as he shoved his hands in the pockets of his crisp dress slacks. "Can I get you something to drink, Rochelle?"

Jayla licked her lips as she stood. She approached him, the look of lust in her eyes revealing her salacious intentions. "As a matter of fact, I am thirsty." She moved slowly and deliberately, her eyes almost daring him to stop her, as she undid his pants. She was satisfied when he didn't move. His pants slid to his ankles, and his dick bounced free from the slit of his boxers. Immediately, she lowered herself to her knees and grasped his meat with her mouth.

"Shit, baby girl," he moaned, his voice low and breathy.

Jayla lathered his dick with so much spit, it started trickling from the corners of her mouth. She sucked and slurped, and the thrill had her own kitty purring to life. His hands grasped the top of her head and fisted in her wig. He drilled deep enough to have her gagging, but she didn't break the rhythm. She felt his tip massage the back of her throat. Giggling at the pleasurable sensation, Jayla used her tongue to stroke his lubricated shaft until it throbbed between her lips.

Grant moaned again, encouraging her to increase her speed. He assaulted her tonsils, and her slurping noises filled the room until he could no longer take it. One final thrust and he emptied his cum on her tongue.

Jayla gargled the cream in her throat before swallowing every drop. For effect, she eyed him seductively as she licked her lips clean. She could feel they had puffed up a bit from the force of the dick sucking.

"Baby girl, baby girl." Grant was sighing in relief as he leaned back on the wall. "I didn't realize how much I needed that."

Jayla rose. "I told you I was thirsty." Not bothering to wait for more, she strutted to the door. Damn, it felt good to be done with this. She couldn't wait to get to the car to call Sheila.

"Wait, Rochelle."

"You take care of yourself, Senator," Jayla called, not bothering to stop or look back. She ignored the receptionist's suspicious frown as she breezed by her glass desk.

Down the elevator and out of the building went Jayla, and she was already punching in Sheila's number as she crossed the parking lot.

Sheila didn't even bother with a greeting when she picked up. "You have something for me?" was all she said.

"Yes," Jayla said. "I just sucked your husband's dick in his office."

Silence. Then Sheila said, "So what?" Her tone was nonchalant. "I'm sure plenty of women have."

Jayla frowned. "So, what the fuck you needed me to do it for?"

"I didn't tell you to suck his dick, Jayla. You did that because you wanted to."

Her amused chuckle had Jayla wishing Sheila was right there in front of her, so she could slap the shit out of her. "Well, what the hell did you need me for, Sheila? I'm tired of these fucking games."

"I'm paying you to help me bring down Senator Weston. You sucking his dick? Big fucking deal. Did you even get it on video?"

"Sheila, you didn't request video." Jayla didn't bother hiding her own annoyance. She just wanted this shit to be over, and it looked like she was running around in circles.

"Well, you got to give me something," Sheila snapped. "Pictures, video, recordings. Something. What the hell is your purpose? I'm supposed to just go on what you tell me happened? Come on now. Step ya game up, Jayla."

The click in her ear had Jayla fuming. She had begun punching the numbers to dial Sheila again when she noticed she'd received a text message from Quentin. Have you talked to Jasmine? No one has heard from her in over a week.

Jayla rolled her eyes and deleted the message. Why the hell should she care? Her phone rang in her hands, and Jayla frowned at the generic collect call number flashing on the screen. She immediately hit DECLINE. Dreena was still on her bullshit, and Jayla didn't have time for it. She would take the hint eventually. But one thing was for sure. Jayla needed to hurry and get Sheila Weston what she wanted, so she could move the fuck on with her life. But something told her this woman would not be easily satisfied.

CHAPTER TWELVE

Jayla

The wedding decorations were tacky.

Jayla frowned as she fingered one of the blue and cream bouquets adorned with ribbons that was tied to the end of each pew. With a glance around, she pulled it off and gained some satisfaction in watching it fall to the floor. She looked up to survey the rest of the sanctuary.

Freddie Jackson's "You Are My Lady" poured through the overhead speakers. Tulle had been hung from the ceiling near the altar to create a canopy, and two pillars stood on either side of it, with silk wedding flowers woven around each one. An aisle runner covered the length of space from the door to the altar, and Jayla couldn't help the sting of hurt when she saw it was customized: TARA AND DERRICK. AND THE TWO SHALL BECOME ONE.

Before Jayla could stop herself, she stooped down and ripped the thin fabric. Guests gasped at her bold act, but she didn't care. "Bitch," she mumbled, snatching off more of the pew decorations. Silk and tulle littered the floor, and Jayla no longer cared about subtlety.

"Hey, stop!" A deep voice she didn't recognize echoed in the sanctuary, and seconds later rough hands snatched Jayla to her feet. A man's frowning face came into view.

"Get your hands off me!" she said, struggling to escape his tight grip on her arms. "This entire wedding is bullshit."

By now, people had begun to gather around, and their disapproving glares were burning into her. Derrick's mom, Gloria, was smirking at her, the curl of her lips conveying something between triumph and "I told you so." Jayla wanted to spit in her damn face.

"I got her," a voice said, and Jayla glanced over as Patricia took her arm. "Let's go, Puma." Her tone was firm as she steered her to the sanctuary doors.

As soon as they had made it outside, Jayla pulled her arm from Patricia's grasp and whirled on her. "What the fuck are you doing here, Patricia?" Her vision was clouded with tears. "You're giving me all that bullshit about leaving Derrick alone and not being hurt, and yet you're here supporting it."

"I'm here supporting Gloria," Patricia said, correcting Jayla, with a glare. "Plus, I had a feeling you would come up here and try something. You always have been stubborn. How the hell did you find out the wedding was today anyway?"

Jayla pulled the crumpled invitation from her pocket and held it up in Patricia's face. "Found this in the trash," she said, hurling the paper to the ground. "Thanks for the heads-up, Patricia."

Patricia sighed. "Leave that man alone, Puma. I've seen the two of them together. He is finally happy. Don't you love him enough to let him be happy?"

Jayla crumpled on the steps and cried into her hands. Her mentor was right, but it still didn't make the ordeal any less painful. The door opened at her back, and rapid footsteps crossed the cement porch. Jayla didn't bother looking over as a woman sat down beside her. Patricia left them alone.

"Why did I know you would try something stupid like this? You just couldn't leave well enough alone," Jackie observed.

Jayla rolled her eyes at her sister's condescending tone. "What the fuck ever, Jackie," she snapped. "I don't expect you to understand, since you and Tara are best friends now."

"Me and Tara have always gotten along. But you really want to talk to me about betrayal? Isn't that the pot calling the kettle black?"

Jayla finally looked over at Jackie. She sat there in her bridesmaid dress. It was a chiffon halter maxi dress, and the periwinkle color looked beautiful against Jackie's bronzed complexion. She had her hair done up to show off the teardrop earrings that glistened in her ears. Even her makeup was tasteful: simplistic but just enough to enhance the squint of her eyes and her deep-set frown.

"You should go," Jackie said. "You ruined so many lives, especially Tara's and Derrick's. You slept with her husband, Jayla. Damn. You cheated on Derrick left, right, and sideways. Do you really think sabotaging this wedding will make him want to have *anything* to do with you?"

Jayla didn't bother responding. She wasn't in the mood for Jackie's logic. Even if it was the truth.

"Exactly," Jackie said, seeming satisfied with Jayla's silence. "So, for once, stop being so fucking selfish. If either one of them sees you here, they'll probably call the police. Grow up and stop acting so damn reckless."

Her sister's calm reasoning was enough to ignite Jayla's anger. "Why are you even out here?" she barked. "You probably would love to see me go back to jail or get myself into some deeper shit. Why are you bothering me with this 'loving my sister' mess, like it even matters to you?"

Shock had Jackie opening her mouth, then closing it again. She shrugged. "To be honest, I don't know. With everything you've done, I should hate you." She sighed and looked out toward the parking lot. "But I don't. No matter how fucked up you are, you're still my sister." She bit off those last words, as if the truth left a bad taste in her mouth.

Jayla expected as much. She doubted they could ever have the same relationship they used to have.

Out of the blue, Jackie asked, "Have you heard from Jasmine?"

Jackie's sudden question had Jayla frowning. "No. Why the hell is everyone asking me that question, like I'm cool with that girl? What's supposed to be going on with her now?"

"She's not answering her phone," Jackie said. "It's not like we talk every day, but it's been nearly a week since I heard her voice. Now her phone is going straight to voicemail. You sure you haven't talked to her?"

"No. Damn, Jackie. Why would I lie about that?"

"I don't know. Considering you snuck behind my back to pimp her out and took her to get an abortion, you really think I can trust you right now? You're both sneaky as hell."

Jayla's sigh was heavy with annoyance. "She's probably in some shit her stupid ass can't get out of. Who knows with her?"

Jackie grunted. "Yeah. Like mother, like daughter."

"You can quit all the nasty little digs at me, Jackie," Jayla murmured, resting her chin in her hands. "You still call yourself pissed at me because I was writing Quentin in jail? It wasn't like you gave a damn about me then, so what does it matter?"

"What? You were writing Quentin in jail?"

"I'm not entertaining his nonsense. So, you don't have to worry about me messing up your marriage." Jayla rose to climb down the steps, and she was surprised when Jackie followed her.

"Jayla, what the hell are you talking about?" Jackie grabbed her wrist and turned her around. "You were writing Quentin in jail? And what do you mean, messing up my marriage?"

Jayla crossed her arms over her chest and studied her sister. Jackie's face reflected the same confusion she, Jayla, felt. "Aren't you getting a divorce?" she said.

"Yeah, but how do you have anything to do with that?"

Jayla was silent, struggling to make sense of everything. Something wasn't adding up. "Why did you two separate?" she asked cautiously.

Anger replaced confusion on Jackie's face, and her eyes narrowed. "I don't want to talk about it. But I still don't see what any of this has to do with you."

Everything. If he is telling the truth. "Did he leave you?" Jayla asked, and with that question, Jackie erupted in laughter.

"Please. I left his sneaky ass."

"He said he left you . . ." Jayla shook her head as she thought to herself, Why would he lie about that?

"He's telling a bald-faced lie," Jackie snapped, as if reading her thoughts. "His nasty . . . You know what? Don't even get me started on that, because I'll get pissed all over again." Jackie turned sharply on her heel and, gathering her dress, stomped up the stairs.

Jayla watched her disappear back into the church. Something wasn't right. She was more pissed at Quentin than Jackie, even though he had indicated he told Jackie about them. Jackie hadn't reacted like she had found their letters. She hadn't reacted like she knew Quentin was leaving her to be with Jayla. She had reacted as if . . .

Jayla pulled out her phone and dialed Quentin's number. It rang twice before going to voicemail. She walked to her car as she typed a quick text message. Call me now. We need to talk. She didn't realize she was headed to his apartment until she had turned onto his street. Jayla didn't know why

Quentin had lied to her, but she was going to get to the bottom of it.

Surprisingly, Quentin was sitting in his car when she pulled into his section of the apartment complex. The windows to his Camry were tinted, but Jayla could easily make out his shadow in the back seat. What the hell was he doing? Since his apartment was situated in a secluded part of the complex, no other cars were in sight.

Jayla parked beside him and got out, then stepped up to one of the Camry's rear windows and squinted through the darkened glass. Her eyes ballooned in horror and her stomach turned at the sight on the other side of the glass. It was definitely Quentin in the back seat, and he was sitting with his head back against the headrest. But a head in his lap was bobbing up and down, generously sucking on Quentin's dick. Even worse, that couldn't be who she thought it was. . . .

Furious, Jayla pounded her palm on the window, startling both of them and bringing a halt to the dick-sucking session. She tried the door, and to her surprise, it was unlocked, so she pulled it open, and confirmed that her eyes weren't deceiving her. The embarrassed expression of Quentin's face only heightened her anger.

"So, this is why Jackie left you!" she yelled, punching Quentin in the jaw.

"Wait a minute," he sputtered, struggling to climb out of the back seat. "It's not what you think." Quentin's feet became twisted in his dangling pant legs, and he tripped and literally fell out of the car. He landed ass up on the pavement, with his pants and boxers tangled around his ankles.

"Not what I *think*!" Jayla screamed as she kicked him in the side. "I think I just saw you getting your dick sucked by a fucking nigga, that is what I think!" She kicked him again. "Is that it, Quentin? You got HIV because you're fucking gay?"

Quentin groaned under the blows of her sneakers as he held up his hands out in surrender.

Jayla kept kicking until she felt two strong hands pull her away from Quentin's limp body. "Get the fuck off me!" she yelled, whirling on the man, her eyes ablaze. "Does Grant know you a dick-in-the-booty nigga? I'm sure that won't go over well in his campaign. Not to mention your new uniform."

Carl dropped his eyes. He had the nerve to be fully dragged out in a fire-red mini tube dress that hugged each of his well-defined muscles. Hairy legs peeked out from beneath the dress, and his feet looked like boats in the matching red heels. The brunette bob wig lay sideways on his head and was matted at the crown, where Quentin had been clutching it. Carl licked his lips nervously, those same lips still swollen from grasping Quentin's dick, and Jayla gagged.

"He doesn't know," Carl admitted. "But he can't find out."

Jayla opened her mouth to ask why, and with disgust, she noticed Carl was fiddling with the wedding band around his finger. She shook her head, looking between the two men, as her chest heaved. Then the idea suddenly materialized in her mind as clearly as if fate had placed it there by hand. She smirked. Maybe this could work in her favor, after all.

"I'll keep your precious secret," she said, her nose so close in Carl's face she could smell the nut on his breath. "But only on one condition."

CHAPTER THIRTEEN

Jayla

Of course he would be late.

Jayla angled her wrist to look at her watch and smacked her lips impatiently. Grant was supposed to be leaving his office for the day, according to the schedule Sheila had given her. His limo was sitting idle by the curb, but still no Grant. And here she was, across the street, perched on a bench, trying not to be obvious, with her magazine open to the same page for the past thirty minutes.

Her phone buzzed, and Jayla snatched her eyes from the office building entrance to dig it out of her purse. She wasn't surprised when she saw Quentin's number flashing on the screen. He was pissed at her and had been blowing her up nonstop. As if his pathetic begging was going to change her mind.

Jayla swiped her finger to reject the incoming call and groaned out loud when her phone immediately rang again. "You're acting like a bitch for real now," she said after answering.

"Man, quit that shit, Jaye," Quentin snapped. "You know what you're doing is fucked up."

"For who, boo? For you? Because you have to share your precious boy toy? Carl definitely didn't seem to mind."

"For Grant. Real talk. Don't do this."

Jayla exaggerated a yawn. "Or what?" she said. "Am I supposed to be scared of you, Quentin?"

"You should be," he replied, his voice lowered. If Jayla had been paying attention, she would've taken heed of the threat.

But her eyes had lifted just in time to see Grant emerge from the building, and she'd jumped to her feet. "Whatever," she said absently. "I need him to finish some business, and I'll be done, so he can jump back in your ass as soon as possible. You have my word."

Before he could respond, Jayla clicked the phone off and walked briskly across the street. Grant was already climbing in the limo, so Jayla quickened her pace. Her eyes took in each of the three men who were accompanying the senator, and sure enough, Carl was not in the mix. *Damn, where is Carl? He is supposed to be stalling Grant. His ass better hold up his end of the bargain.*

Without thinking, Jayla raised her voice so she would be heard over the downtown traffic and called, "Grant!" When Grant looked up, Jayla raised her hand and waved. She noticed his lips curve slightly, and she grinned. She just needed one more night. One more night and her plan would be set.

Jayla's breath caught in her throat when she was suddenly snatched from behind and slammed back first into the concrete beneath her feet. Stabbing pain penetrated her bones and had a hiss erupting from between her clenched teeth. She didn't have time to register what had happened before several figures came into view. She opened her mouth to speak, and a fist to her face snatched the question from her lips. A combination of fists and sneakers began pummeling her from every angle, and Jayla attempted to shield herself from the beating. Tears stung her cheeks as her body burned with pain. Her stomach, her legs, face. It was as if her skin was splitting open with each blow.

"Stop!" she cried. "Please!" Her vision wavered, then clouded, and she felt as if she was on the edges of death. Then she went numb.

Voices were yelling at her, but they sounded like distant whispers. "That's for Dreena, bitch. She's getting out soon, and she's coming for that ass."

One more punch and the darkness swallowed her.

***

Machines hummed in the background and nearly drowned out the hushed voices. Jayla kept her eyes shut, struggling to take her mind off the dull throbbing in her head and the pain blanketing her body.

"Damaged," someone murmured. "Fractures . . . bruising . . ." The snatches of conversation were jumbled and fuzzy. Either that or the throbbing in her head was making everything incoherent. Jayla moaned and winced as the sounds echoed loudly in her ears.

The talking stopped. "Rochelle?"

Is that Grant? Jayla lifted her heavy lids and squinted, and soon the room came into focus. Sure enough, Grant stood at the foot of the bed, worry creasing his face. A man in a lab coat stood on the left side of the hospital bed. Jayla opened her mouth to speak, but she didn't have the energy to utter anything but another moan.

"I'm Dr. Wise," the other man said, pulling a light pen from the pocket of his lab coat. "I just want you to take a few moments to relax. We're going to run some tests to make sure nothing is broken or injured."

He flashed the light in each eye, and it was enough to blind her temporarily. She sucked in a breath as spots danced in front of her eyes, and then she squeezed her lids shut, wishing she had the energy to cuss him out.

"She may have a slight concussion," Dr. Wise said. "We're going to run a few tests, and we'll get you all squared away." He offered a comforting smile and a pat to her leg before he left the room.

Jayla found enough strength to look around the room and was grateful when she realized that she and Grant were now alone. Grant stepped over to the side of the bed and took Jayla's hand. The gesture shocked both of them.

"How are you feeling?" he asked.

"Like hell," she murmured with a sigh.

Grant nodded. "That's understandable. You got messed up pretty bad."

Embarrassment colored Jayla's cheeks. She glanced away from his questioning stare. "I think they were trying to rob me," she said. It was a weak excuse, but it was a believable one.

Grant opened his mouth to speak but stopped short when the door opened.

Carl didn't bother looking at Jayla as he entered the room. "Sir, Mrs. Weston is on the phone. She insists it's urgent."

"Tell her we'll meet up later."

"Grant," Jayla said. "Go ahead. I'll be fine."

Grant hesitated, obviously torn about leaving Jayla's side. "I just want to make sure you're okay," he said.

"I'm fine. They're just going to do some tests and probably give me some medicine to knock me out. Please go ahead. I promise I'll be fine." Jayla blew a sigh of relief when Grant nodded. She didn't need him hanging around and finding out something that could ruin everything.

Grant gestured in her direction, and obediently, Carl pulled out a business card and crossed the room to lay it on the bedside table. Jayla found it amusing that he still made a point not to make eye contact.

"I put my personal cell on the back," Grant told her. "Please call me if you need anything." He smiled one last time before he and Carl left the room.

The X-rays revealed she just had some bruising, but nothing was broken, thank God. Jayla sat up in the bed, partially numb from the drugs she'd been given but beyond pissed at Dreena's cowardly ass. She was one of those chicks who got her ratchet bitches to handle her dirty work. The bad thing was that Dreena's childish bullshit had knocked Jayla off schedule. Her job for Sheila was supposed to be over today. Sheila had made it more obvious how time sensitive this assignment was.

Jayla was determined to cooperate with her doctor and the nurses so she would be released from the hospital as soon as possible. No one needed to know she had gotten her ass royally handed to her on a silver platter. So, when she was wheeled back to her room after a CT scan, she was surprised to find Jackie sitting on the couch. She groaned inwardly. Damn. This was not what she needed. Who the hell had even contacted Jackie?

Jackie waited as the two hospital staff members transferred Jayla from the wheelchair back to the bed. As soon as the door clicked closed behind them, she stood and moseyed over to the side of the bed. Jayla felt her sister's eyes scrutinizing her, and she turned away. She hadn't bothered looking at herself in a mirror since she'd been admitted to the hospital, but her face felt tight, so she knew the swelling had to be bad. She knew she looked awful.

"I see you finally got what you deserved," Jackie said.

Jayla would've rolled her eyes if the gesture didn't hurt. She struggled to rearrange the covers with the one arm she could still use. She wasn't surprised when her sister just watched her and didn't bother to help. "What do you want?" she muttered. "Who the hell called you anyway?"

Jackie crossed her arms over her large breasts. "Patricia."

Patricia? Jayla frowned, trying to remember if Patricia had been anywhere around Grant's office building at the time she was assaulted. *No, of course not*, she decided. "How does Patricia know I'm here?"

Jackie threw up her hands. "Shit, I don't know Jayla. She called me, and I came right over here.

Does it really matter? You lucky I came in the first place."

"Gee, thanks." Jayla's response was as dry as her throat. "I was robbed. But thank you so much for your sympathy, big sis." It was becoming too painful to talk, so Jayla let out an exhausted sigh and lay back on the stiff mattress.

"Are they admitting you?" Jackie's voice had softened a degree.

"No." In reality, Jayla didn't know if they were or not, but she damn sure wouldn't be staying. She had shit to do. "I found out about Quentin," she said, remembering the sickening visual.

Jackie smacked her teeth. "He told you, huh?"

"No, I saw that shit."

"Fucking down-low bastard. Whatever. I'm better off without him." She turned and walked toward the window.

Jayla couldn't tell if she was crying or not. "How was the wedding?" she asked, changing the subject.

Jackie chuckled. "If you're asking me if they still got married despite you trying to fuck that up, the answer is yes."

And there they went. Riding off into the sunset on some happily fucking ever after. Jayla didn't know if she wanted to cry, break something, or throw up the stale bologna sandwich a nurse had brought her to snack on.

"I need to pee," Jackie said, heading toward Jayla's bathroom. "Be right back." She stepped into the small bathroom and shut the door behind her, leaving Jayla alone with her thoughts.

Just then there was a knock on the door, and Dr. Wise entered with a clipboard in hand. "How are you feeling, Ms. Morgan?" he asked with a smile.

Jayla nodded. "Much better," she lied.

"That's good to hear. Well, it looks like no serious damage. Now, you've got some bumps and bruises, and you'll probably feel like crap for a few days, while you heal. But I've prescribed some antibiotics and painkillers, so you should be just fine."

"Great. Thank you."

The doctor turned to leave, then turned back around. "Oh yeah," he added after glancing back at the papers on his clipboard. "I'm going to prescribe you some more Atripla. Your T cell count is a little low. You should definitely be more careful, considering your diagnosis."

Jayla felt her heart stop as the doctor left the room. Had Jackie heard that?

As if on cue, Jackie emerged from the bathroom, her eyes boring into Jayla's. *Shit.* She had never told anyone about her HIV.

"Um, what was that about?" Jackie asked. When Jayla turned up her lips in confusion, Jackie shook her head. "Don't even part your lips to lie to me, Jayla. Damn. What the hell was the doctor talking about? What diagnosis?"

Jayla felt her breath roaring in her ears. Suddenly, she forgot all her pain, just saw the suspicion etched on her sister's face. *Shit, shit, shit. What to say?*

"You might as well tell me the truth," Jackie said, as if reading her sister's mind. She pulled her cell phone from the pocket of her jacket. "Won't take me but a second to Google that medication. What did he say? Atripla?"

Damn. She was right. Jayla's sigh was heavy from reluctance. "All right," she said. "I have HIV." Shame had her refusing to look at her sister.

Jackie's hesitation was long and calculated. When she finally spoke, her tone had no emotion attached to it. "How long have you had it?"

"A long time. But I just found out about it." Jayla watched her sister pace in front of the bed.

"A long time, huh?" Jackie stopped and leaned against the bed. "How long is a long time, Jayla?"

"What difference does it make? I tell you I'm fucking dying, and you grilling me on how long I've had it?"

Jayla's outburst didn't faze Jackie one bit. She continued to stare, and it was evident her mind was racing. "Who did you get it from?"

Jayla frowned to mask her fear. "How the hell should I know, Jackie?" she said, raising her voice from agitation. "You, of all people, should know how many niggas I slept with, remember? You make sure to remind me every chance you get."

"Damn, Jayla! Do you know how to open your mouth and say *anything* other than a lie?" Jackie yelled, gripping the bed rail until her knuckles were sheet white. "Stop playing me for a fucking idiot."

"What are you talking about?"

"I know Quentin has HIV!" Jackie was all but screaming across the room. "Now, let the shit out. Did you give it to him? Did he give it to you? Or is it just a small fucking world, after all?"

Jayla's mouth shuddered open as tears brimmed in her eyes. Jackie had tried to kill her once. The bitch was liable to fillet her ass around all these hospital tools. Desperate, Jayla quickly pressed the HELP button to summon the nurse as her thoughts stumbled on top of each other.

"Get out," she said.

Jackie nodded. Her sister's reaction was evidence enough. "You *did* fuck him." Her voice was amazingly calm as she spoke. "I knew it. So, it's true. Jasmine is your and his child."

Jayla didn't even bother asking her how she knew. It didn't even matter. What mattered now was that the pieces were snapping neatly into place. And what the hell would her sister do, now that she saw the big picture?

The giggle started first, a low sound that had Jayla wondering if she had even heard anything at all. She looked up, and sure enough, Jackie's lips were pursed together as she struggled to maintain her composure. Giggles seeped through her lips before she lost it and burst into all-out laughter. Jayla held her breath. Jackie had clearly had lost it.

"I don't believe this shit," Jackie said between gasps as she wiped the tears from her eyes. "So, all that shit was for nothing. Nothing. Just to raise you and my husband's love child? You got to be fucking kidding me."

She continued to laugh hysterically, and Jayla pressed the HELP button once more, not knowing or caring what the hell her sister was talking about.

"Everything I did for that child? Everything I did, and I find *this* out? This shit is funny as hell!"

She was clearly delirious. Jayla could only sigh in relief when the door to her hospital room opened.

The nurse crossed the floor with a smile. "Great timing," she said. "I was on my way to give you a message. Some cop was looking for you."

Jayla froze. As if on cue, Heather arresting her in the airport played like a scene from a movie in her head. Damn! Had Sheila reneged on their deal? "Cop?" she repeated.

"Yes, ma'am, and he was too fine." She busied herself with fluffing Jayla's pillows as Jayla slid a look to her sister. Jackie watched quietly.

"What did he want?" Jayla asked, and the nurse gave a half-hearted shrug.

"Not sure. Something about your mother's case. I told him you were resting and to come back later."

Jayla felt like she had swallowed lead. *Her mother's case. Shit.* What the hell had happened to make that resurface? And to cause the officer to come looking for her? Fear had stiffened her neck to the point that it had begun to hurt. She let out a shuddering sigh and looked away to avoid Jackie's questioning stare. She just knew shit was going to get worse before it got any better.

CHAPTER FOURTEEN

Jayla

After being in a coma for two days, fourteen-year-old Jayla was disoriented and felt that her brain was about as useful as mashed potatoes. She couldn't remember a thing. All she knew was she was in severe pain and now had a razor-thin scar along her bikini line from the apparent C-section. She remembered she had been pregnant. That much was certain. Everything else was fuzzy.

"I'm so happy you're okay," her mother, Jillian, said as she drove. "You definitely had us all worried."

Jayla turned to look at her mother's profile. The mahogany complexion, the wild mane of gentle curls were mirror images of her own, with the exception of the blond highlights in her hair. She had Jillian's eyes too. They were . . . unreadable right now, as they remained focused on the road ahead. Jayla couldn't help feeling that something wasn't right. But what? She didn't know. She touched her stomach, which was still inflated from the baby it had recently carried.

"It was for the best," Jillian said, noticing the absentminded gesture.

"What?"

"The adoption," she replied, clarifying. "It was for the best. It was what you wanted."

Was it? Jayla didn't remember, but it sounded like the truth.

When they got home, Jocelyn and Aunt Bev bombarded her with questions she didn't know the answers to. The shit frustrated her so much that she finally locked herself in her bedroom and cried empty tears, which she couldn't rationalize.

At one point, her mother knocked on the door. "I'm putting some food and your meds out here, Jaye," she said, her voice muffled.

Grateful, Jayla dragged herself from the bed. She was having cramps, and there was a dull throbbing around the tender flesh of her incision. She retrieved her hydrocodone and popped two pills. The lemonade tasted bitter as she washed the medicine down, but she emptied the glass, nonetheless. That was when a cloudy memory began to materialize, as if someone was focusing a lens.

"Que," she murmured and reached for the phone. She remembered her boyfriend, her love. The fa-

ther of her baby. How could she forget? He could help her fill in the blanks. She was too excited, or maybe that part of her mind was still hazy, but it took her seven tries to get all the digits right.

Quentin picked up on the first ring. "What?" he snapped into the phone.

"Babe, I—"

"Don't call me that."

Confusion had Jayla at a loss for words. "Que, what is the matter?"

"Don't call me anymore," he replied in a hushed tone. "What we had was a mistake. You know I'm with your sister."

His words were like a light bulb, and the rest of her memories came tumbling down on her like a stack of bricks.

She'd had sex with her sister's boyfriend. She'd gotten pregnant with his baby. She had wanted it. She loved him. Why not share a part of him? He was pissed. He loved Jackie. She, too, was pregnant with his child. That was the life he wanted. An argument with her mother. She knew about the affair with Quentin. Jayla didn't care. Jillian had already tried to push abortion, but with Jayla now thirty-six weeks along, that was clearly out of the question. Adoption was the one and only option, because her mother had insisted she couldn't keep the baby. Jayla knew the bitch was crazy, and she had continued to eat her dinner, ignoring her. Then the contractions had started, had become so intense, until she had collapsed on the floor in excruciating pain. She remembered Jillian hadn't moved from her place at the table, had merely watched her writhe in pain as she slipped a pill bottle into her purse.

Jayla stood, the phone slipping from her weak fingers, as she processed everything. Her mother had given her something. What, she didn't know. But whatever it was, it had pushed her into labor and subsequently a coma. She had almost died. And for what? So Jillian could give her baby away? So, there would be no proof of her affair with Quentin?

Jayla walked out of her bedroom, fueled by a seething anger, and stumbled down the hall. The betrayal cut deep, and the hurt from the wound was intense enough to bring tears to her eyes.

"Jaye?" Her mother's voice stopped her in her tracks.

"It's me," she answered.

Jillian appeared in the doorway at the end of the hall, already in her pajamas, a bottle of Grey Goose in her hand. She looked as if she had been crying. "I'm glad you're up and at 'em again," she said, brandishing a small smile. "Do you think you can bring me something to drink, so I can take my medicine?"

"Sure." Jayla's word came out in a whisper. She made her way to the staircase and started down, but shock left her planted on the bottom steps. How could her mother be so vindictive? How could you have done what she did?

Jayla didn't remember going into the kitchen or pouring a glass of grape juice. But she did remember standing there and staring down into the liquid, her vision blurred from her emotions. Her nails bit into her right palm, and Jayla opened her clenched fist to see what was the matter. The hydrocodone pill bottle glistened from the sweat on her hand.

She didn't even think. Even as she poured the entire bottle of pills into the juice, then watched them fizz as they dissolved, all she saw was her mother watching her as she lay writhing on the dining room floor from the painful contractions. Jayla dipped her finger in the juice and stirred until there were no remnants of the pills or any residue left. Jayla carried the glass upstairs.

Jillian lay in the dark but for the eerie light cast by the episode of The Fresh Prince of Bel Air *on the television. Her mother sat against her headboard, nursing her alcohol.*

Jayla placed the glass on her nightstand, next to the Goody's Headache Powder. Jillian was notorious for drinking heavy alcohol at night and chasing it with aspirin so she wouldn't have a hangover.

"Jaye." Jillian's voice was soft. "I'm so sorry about what happened. But I promise. I am so glad you're alive and okay. I know this has been traumatic, but we'll get through this, baby."

Jayla lowered her head. Maybe, just maybe, it wasn't true. Maybe her mother loved her, despite their constant arguments. Maybe the trauma of her ordeal had her hallucinating. But maybe not.

"Mama." Jayla kept her back to her. "Did you do this to me?"

There it was. The long pause that confirmed all her suspicions. Jillian had taken her Goody's and polished off her juice to keep from answering. And Jayla hadn't bothered stopping her. She meant only to make Jillian sick. Worst-case scenario, nausea would put her mother in the hospital for a few days.

But the next morning, after having choked on her own vomit from a toxic combination of alcohol and hydrocodone, Jayla had been stricken with guilt. That was the first time she had attempted suicide. And even worse, she had confessed to Quentin.

Jayla couldn't sleep. The memory was as fresh as if she was watching it play on a screen. After she had feigned intense pain, thankfully, the doctor had insisted Jackie leave her hospital room.

And with everything going on, Jayla had been glad. She had needed time to think about what the hell was going on. Now she was at home, and a few days had passed since she was discharged from the hospital.

The gist of what was happening was still surreal. They were reopening her mother's case, all over an anonymous tip. And she had a pretty good idea who would've tipped them off. Damn, she had fucked up by telling Quentin. She knew even then that it was probably a mistake. But she had been riddled with grief and teetering on the edges of insanity. He had talked her off the ledge. He had promised to take the secret to his grave as long as she backed off.

"Jackie just had our baby girl, Jasmine," he'd explained. "Let us have our life." Of course, she hadn't put two and two together and determined that this baby was really hers. But how could she have known? Jackie had been pregnant, too. Jayla hadn't known about Jackie's miscarriage, and her mother had claimed that she gave Jayla's baby up for adoption. Which was the reason she was buried six feet under. So Jayla had agreed to back off and had been assured that all would be well.

So why was she now a person of interest in a case that had long ago been put to rest? *Because Quentin is a pussy that couldn't keep his damn mouth shut.* Jayla rolled her eyes. He had pulled a bitch move in tipping off the police because she was using his butt-fuck Carl. His precious feelings were hurt. And now she could do some hard time if the police pursued the case. Not the little Fisher-Price time she had done before. No, hard time. Prison. A murder conviction could have her ass gone so long she would need Depends by the time she saw the light of day again.

Jayla rolled over and peeked at the clock on the nightstand. Four fifty-two a.m. It was early, but she didn't care. She had to get on it if she was going to untangle herself from this mess. Starting with Grant and Sheila Weston. She was still sore, and her skin had turned colors with the aging bruises, but she needed it to go down tonight.

The hotel suite was the best way. Jayla had booked a gorgeous suite overlooking downtown Atlanta and had called Grant. She had made up some excuse about being unable to sleep in her own bed because of nightmares from the attack, and he had insisted on rushing right over. She had shot Carl a text, and now everything was pretty much ready.

Jayla pulled a few clothes from her suitcase and placed them strategically on the chair and floor. She gave the room a last once-over before she headed to the bar to pour their drinks. When she was about to pass the mirror near the entrance to the suite, Jayla stopped to observe herself. Even with the swelling and the purple and blue bruises peppering her skin, she knew she looked damn good. The black lingerie set was see-through, affording a delicious display of her nipples and the G-string nestled between her cheeks. Grant had seen her without the wig after her ass whupping, so she hadn't bothered with it today, instead letting her natural mane fly free. Jayla drew in a nervous breath and continued to the bar. She hoped everything fell into place like she wanted it to.

She had just poured herself some sangria when a knock came at the door. She took her time sipping from the wineglass, and when she had finished, she poured herself some more. Then, after grabbing Grant's drink, she carried both glasses to the door and swung it open.

"Hey," she greeted.

Grant stepped over the threshold, then shrugged out of his blazer. He was dressed comfortably in a T-shirt and khakis, and Jayla had to admire how the pants fit snug around his thighs. "What is it?" he asked when she continued to stare.

"I was just wondering if you own a pair of jeans," Jayla answered with a smile.

Grant chuckled. "No, not really. Glad to see you're doing a little better."

"A little." She sighed for effect. "I'm sorry to bring you out so late. I was just lonely and probably a little paranoid."

"No, no, I understand. It's okay." Grant nudged the door closed behind him and gave Jayla a reassuring kiss on the cheek.

Jayla had to admit, she was grateful for his compassion. She handed him his glass and took another sip of her own drink. "I can't believe I'm having nightmares, like some little girl." She chuckled, leading the way to the bed. "You would think my grown ass knew how to handle this kind of thing."

Grant eyed the cluster of candles lit by the bed and sniffed the pleasant smell of lavender and vanilla hanging in the air. "You always sleep with candles lit?" he questioned.

"I like the way they smell."

He nodded, taking another gulp from his drink, sat down on the edge of the bed, and toed off his shoes. It was then Jayla noticed how stressed he appeared to be. He suddenly looked older, the deep creases in his face seeming more prominent. She sat down beside him and watched him stare off into the distance.

"What's the matter?" she asked, rubbing his leg.

He sighed. "I found out some news that is really bothering me. About Marcus."

Jayla felt her heart skip a beat. "What kind of news?"

"That his car accident may have been . . ." He paused and cleared his throat. "May have been foul play."

Jayla nodded, smiling inwardly at his slight slur. She studied his pupils and the first few beads of sweat dotting his forehead. The roofies were taking affect faster than she had expected. She rushed to coax more information out of him before he was too gone. "Now what? Are you going to go to the police?"

"Dunno," Grant mumbled with a yawn. "I'm so mad. She said she loved me."

"Who?" Jayla asked, but Grant just shook his head. "Who, Grant?" She watched Grant's head loll forward and his chin rest on his chest as he volleyed between staying awake and going to sleep. Jayla opened her mouth to ask again. Then shut it. How much did he know? she wondered. And what was he planning on doing with the information?

Putting that out of her mind, Jayla smiled and scooted closer, until their hips and thighs touched. "Grant, I need you, baby," she whispered close to his ear. "I can't stop thinking about you. Show me how much you've missed me." With that, she crushed her lips to his.

His response was immediate, and he lifted his hand to grab her breasts. He pushed her back on the bed and threw his leg over her lap. The drugs had his aggression on ten, and he poured so much passion into the kiss that Jayla felt like he was trying to kiss her soul. His thick tongue tangled with hers, and his lips bruised her swollen ones in a pleasantly painful massage.

The taste of alcohol was heavy on his breath as their saliva mixed. She sighed, already feeling the sensitive flesh between her thighs growing damp. Then she heard a beeping sound that was so low it was barely audible, and this was followed by a quick flash of light. This had her prolonging the kiss. Satisfied that the kiss was long enough, she rolled on top of him, ignoring the burst of pain that shot across her ribs. She undid his pants with rapid fingers, wrapped her lips around his dick, and took it all in, in one juicy mouthful.

Jayla took her time sucking, allowing Grant to tangle his fingers in her hair as she polished his shaft. She eyed him and smiled to herself when his lids fell shut. She gave one final flick of her tongue over his tip before sitting up to her knees. He hadn't cum yet. But he was nearly trembling with desire.

"Grant," she whispered, watching his head roll from side to side. "I want to do something with you. Would you like that?"

His response was a groan, as his lips were too heavy to form a coherent word.

Jayla looked toward the closet door, which was already slight ajar, and motioned toward it.

"Now?" Carl whispered as he peeked his head through.

Jayla glanced at Grant again. "Yeah, he's out of it good," she said, climbing to her feet.

When Carl approached the bed, she held out her hand for the digital camera he was holding. "Now. Your turn." When he hesitated, Jayla sucked her teeth and slapped her hand on her hip. "I know your rainbow ass don't call yourself getting a fucking conscience." She couldn't help but notice how pathetic the man looked as he shifted from foot to foot. He was probably blushing in embarrassment, but it wasn't noticeable on his midnight-black complexion. Immediately, her mind flashed to the image of this same man, who was now standing in front of her in some jeans and a button-up, dressed as a woman in that damn red minidress and size fourteen heels. That bullshit she had seen with Quentin she knew she could never unsee, and it made her sick to her stomach all over again.

"Did you bring your work clothes?" Jayla asked, her face wrinkled in disgust. "I want both pictures."

He nodded. "Jayla, Grant is a cool dude." He was almost whining. "I really don't want—"

"I don't give a fuck what you want," Jayla snapped, her eyes rounded in impatience. "Get over there so we can take these pictures and go.

Damn! You want to maintain your image, but you need a pussy to go with those dresses you wear, Carl."

Without another word, Carl handed her the camera and positioned himself between Grant's legs. The sight of Carl's big ass sucking Grant's dick was utterly disgusting, but Jayla just shook her head and began snapping pictures. When Grant began moaning and thrusting his hips forward to meet Carl's lips, Jayla switched to video. Sheila would love this.

"F-f-fuck," Grant slurred as he face-fucked Carl. It didn't take him long before his nut exploded, and Carl swallowed, then licked the white residue from his lips.

Jayla stopped recording and nodded at the footage. "Good job. You a nasty muthafucka, but that shit will stay between us." She gestured toward the closet. "Switch it up, rainbow."

Carl didn't utter a word as he retrieved a duffel bag from the closet. He disappeared into the bathroom, and a few minutes later, he returned in a tight purple halter dress and the same bob wig as before.

Jayla smirked as she prepped the camera once more. "Lie next to him," she instructed. "Look like you're sleep."

Carl moved to the bed and lay next to Grant and rested his hand on the man's chest. Instinctively,

Grant's arm wrapped around Carl's shoulders, and a subconscious smile played on his lips as he fingered the wig. He hadn't moved from the position he was in before, so he was still sprawled on the bed, legs open, his now semi-limp dick lying on his thigh, slick with spit and cum.

Jayla began snapping pictures. "Now touch his dick."

Carl's hand grabbed Grant's shaft and clutched it while Jayla snapped some more pictures. The gesture had Grant moaning in lust and turning toward Carl. He murmured something; then his light snore filled the room.

"Okay," Jayla said, smiling in satisfaction. "We're good."

Carl pulled himself gently from the snuggle, and Grant didn't so much as stir. "You didn't get my face, did you?" he asked. "You said you wouldn't get my face."

"No. Just to be sure, I'll use a blur so there is no way to tell it was you."

"And the money?"

Jayla walked over to her purse, which she'd left on the bar, and pulled out a check. She held it out to him. "Oh, and by the way, you better convince Quentin to leave me the fuck alone. I don't give a damn how much you need to stuff his little booty hole. Tell him he needs to back the fuck up off me and keep his ass away from the police. Or both of your asses will be splashed across the AJC. Understand?"

Carl's eyes clouded with confusion, but he merely nodded and took the check. He didn't even bother changing; he quickly gathered his things and left the hotel suite.

Jayla quickly cleaned up and tossed on some sweatpants and a sweatshirt. She was glad the job was done, because she had more important things to take care of now.

CHAPTER FIFTEEN

Jayla

"Good evening, Ms. Morgan. This is Officer Davis again. Ms. Morgan, it is imperative that I speak with you as soon as possible."

Jayla deleted the message with an agitated roll of her eyes. She wanted to kill Quentin for opening up this can of worms. The constant run-ins with her past, not to mention with the law, were pissing her all the way off. She moved to the bay window and peeked out.

The sun was just beginning to set, giving the sky an orange-tinted background for the clouds drifting by. On the road beyond the driveway, cars whizzed by, but still no sign of Sheila. She wished like hell the woman would hurry the hell up, so they could be all the way done with this.

Jayla went downstairs and into the living room. She was surprised to see Patricia seated on the couch. She hadn't been out of her bedroom too much lately, and watching the woman she loved waste away was making Jayla's heart ache. But she struggled to remain in positive spirits. Patricia had definitely lost some weight, and the satin robe hung off her body. Without the added enhancement of makeup, which she rarely seemed to wear anymore, her features appeared sunken, and her face completely hollow.

"Patricia?" Jayla joined her on the couch and put her arm around the woman's hunched shoulders. "You okay?"

Patricia took a labored breath and forced a small smile. She held up the envelope containing the pictures Jayla had taken of Grant, which she'd taken a look at. "So, you did it."

"Of course. Did you actually doubt me?" Jayla teased.

"Not for a second. Look who taught you." They shared a laugh. "So, Sheila is on her way to pick these up, and then . . . that's it, huh?"

"That's it," Jayla said and sighed in relief. She was beyond thrilled to be finally done with this. Now she could take her money and focus her efforts elsewhere.

Patricia handed Jayla the envelope and climbed to her feet. She moved as if it hurt—going slowly and dragging her feet—as she shuffled toward the kitchen. She looked like crystal. Jayla was surprised at her own simile, but it seemed to fit. Patricia appeared both fragile and pale. This wasn't the Patricia she knew, and it felt weird to see her looking so feeble.

Headlights flashed through the blinds, and eagerly, Jayla trotted to the front door, but not before placing the envelope on the side table in the living room. She pulled the door open and watched Sheila emerge from a crisp white Jaguar, putting a cigarette to her lips. Damn, she changed cars like she changed her panties.

"My, my, my," Sheila called as she tossed the cigarette butt on the driveway and tapped it with the toe of her shoe. "You certainly don't need any more of my money, Ms. Morgan. Looks like you're doing very well for yourself."

"It's a friend's."

"Oh, I know. Don't worry. I won't hold it against you. You give me what I want, so you deserve every dime," Sheila said as she headed up the driveway.

Jayla smirked. "I know. Come in."

Sheila stepped up onto the porch and squinted at Jayla in the porch light. "What the hell happened to your face?"

"Nothing." Jayla stepped to the side to allow the woman to enter the foyer. Her bruises were fading but still very visible against her complexion.

She led the way into the living room and over to the computer she'd placed on the side table. The video was already set up. Jayla picked up the envelope from the table and handed it to her. "Some pictures," she explained as Sheila pulled the prints from the envelope.

Sheila's smile was triumphant as she thumbed through each sickening photo. "Impressive," she murmured, more to herself than to Jayla.

Jayla clicked the PLAY button on the computer, and the video rolled.

Carl's sucking sounds blared from the speakers, and Sheila's eyes widened in amusement. "*Very* impressive, Jayla. Job well done."

Jayla sighed in relief. "So now what?"

Sheila reached in her purse and opened her checkbook. "Now I'll handle the rest," she said, scribbling on a check with a flourish.

"So, that's it?" Jayla asked. just to make sure.

Sheila tore the check along the perforated line and held it up. "For now," she said with a suspicious smile.

The way she said that had Jayla's eyebrows lifting. What was that supposed to mean?

The crash startled them both. Jayla sidestepped Sheila and ran into the kitchen.

"Patricia!" she yelled.

Silence.

"She's over here." Sheila had rounded the island, had stooped down, and was out of sight.

Jayla followed her voice and found Patricia sprawled, unconscious, on the floor, amid droplets of blood and shattered glass.

"Oh my God!" Sheila exclaimed, and her panic-stricken face had Jayla freezing in place. "Jayla. Call an ambulance."

Obediently, Jayla snatched her cell phone from her pocket. For the first time since her sister had been attacked, she prayed hard. She didn't know what she would do if she lost Patricia.

It had been hours since they had wheeled Patricia into the emergency room, and the passage of time was eating at Jayla. Plus, Jayla couldn't help feeling nauseated by the déjà vu of it all. She remembered sitting in this same waiting room almost two years ago. She had been surrounded by everyone she had loved and betrayed: Jackie, Jasmine, Tara, Derrick. . . . And she had struggled to handle the guilt from the fact that she was the reason her sister Jocelyn was there in the first place. Now Jayla shifted on the uncomfortable lobby chair, with only Sheila to keep her from feeling completely alone. And this bitch she didn't trust.

"What the hell is taking so long?" Restless, Jayla climbed to her feet for the umpteenth time and began pacing once more.

Sheila blew out a lazy stream of cigarette smoke, which drifted right below the NO SMOKING sign on the wall. She seemed bored with the situation as she thumbed through the glossy pages of a magazine on her lap.

Jayla smacked her lips and shook her head. She didn't know why she had expected a show of sympathy from Sheila. The woman was as coldhearted as they came. She resumed sitting and rested her forehead in her hands. *They're just getting Patricia situated in a room*, she thought, trying to comfort herself. *She is conscious and doing just fine. She has to be.*

"Is someone here for Patricia Dixon?"

The voice had Jayla jumping to her feet and rushing over to meet the young Hispanic doctor. "I'm here for Patricia. How is she?"

"Were you aware Patricia had cancer?" The doctor's rich Spanish accent coated each word of her question.

"Yes."

"I'm sorry. Patricia died a few moments ago . . ."

The woman's lips kept moving, but Jayla didn't hear a sound. The waiting room seemed to spin, and she shut her eyes to block out the harsh reality. *Dead? Patricia is dead?* Sadness washed over her until it clogged her throat, choking the breath from her lungs.

"Fuck you! Fuck your lying ass! You retarded doctors don't know shit!" It took a minute for Jayla to realize the harsh obscenities were coming from her own trembling lips.

"Jayla, stop." Sheila was at her side, clutching her arm.

Instinct had Jayla turning into her and sobbing on her shoulder.

At a loss, Sheila gave her back an awkward pat. "Hey, I know this is hard for you," she said. "But you've got to be strong. In fact, I'll handle all the arrangements for you. I didn't really know her, but if she was friends with you, then I want to help."

Jayla nodded, grateful for the gesture. She couldn't tell if Sheila's words were even genuine, but at that point, she didn't care. She was completely alone in the world now, and it was comforting to have someone in her corner.

But then her mind wandered to a more critical issue, and she began to panic. *Patricia is dead. Where the hell does that leave me*? she thought. Patricia's death was another tragedy in a long series of traumatic events she had endured, and it was sure to reignite her clinical depression. And that was serious enough to send her to a psychiatric ward.

Jayla was too busy crying to notice Sheila signaling to some figure who had been sitting across the lobby all the while.

CHAPTER SIXTEEN

Jayla

The feel of death was so thick, it nearly suffocated her. Jayla shuddered, struggling to warm her body as an eerie chill prickled her skin, causing goose bumps to rise. She had never before been alone in Patricia's bedroom. Now, in her mentor's absence, all eight hundred square feet of the elaborate master suite felt like a casket.

Jayla emptied the dresser drawers and placed silk blouses and cashmere sweaters in neat stacks on the bed. She didn't know what she was going to do with all of Patricia's things. But she figured packing all the contents of the house was the least she could do.

Sheila had graciously taken care of everything, like she had promised. Patricia had written out some final requests, one of which was that she wished to have her body cremated. Jayla had objected at first. She couldn't stomach the thought of her mentor being reduced to ashes. In the end, however, this request reinforced the finality of Patricia's death, and Jayla viewed it as one more reason for her to pack her stuff and get the hell out of Atlanta.

"Shit." Jayla had been so wrapped up in her thoughts that she had pulled the nightstand drawer completely out of the stand. Its contents had spilled onto the floor. She stooped down to pick up the papers littering the carpet. A receipt caught her eye, and Jayla lifted it closer to her face, frowning at the aged font. A casino receipt. She didn't even know Patricia had gambled. But more evidence of this habit was scattered on the floor: receipts from numerous casinos and horse tracks, losing scratch-off tickets, losing betting stubs, and numerous withdrawal statements and credit-card cash advances.

Jayla sat back on her heels, in shock. Damn, Patricia hadn't just gambled. She'd had a full-fledged addiction. She owed everybody. The name Big D was scrawled across multiple check stubs. There was no telling how many other loan sharks she had borrowed from. She had started to pull out the other nightstand drawer to investigate further when her phone stopped her short. She pulled it from her back pocket and swiped the screen to answer.

"Hello?"

Silence.

Jayla looked at the screen and saw that no call was connected. She rolled her eyes. Dropped calls. Her phone immediately rang again, and she answered it once more. This time, she saw the timer on the touch screen indicating the call was connected, but after saying hello, she was again met with silence. "Hello? Who is this?" Jayla struggled to keep from getting agitated.

More silence, and then the call disconnected. She didn't know if there was some kind of connection issue or if the person on the other end had indeed been fucking with her. She needed a break. All of this was just too much.

Jayla left Patricia's bedroom and made her way downstairs, and her footsteps seemed to echo even louder in the large house. She squeezed back more tears. It felt like just yesterday they were sharing breakfast in the kitchen or making love in the sunroom. Patricia was more than a lover. More than a mentor or a mother figure. The loss of her friendship was probably what hurt the most.

Jayla left the house and meandered down the driveway to retrieve the mail from the mailbox. It was a little warm for the middle of November, but it felt much better than being in that stuffy house. The night was still. Not even a breeze seemed to rustle the trees, so it almost felt as if the air stood frozen. Jayla felt numb as she hiked to the mailbox, yanked it open, and pulled out the mail. She thumbed through second- and third-notice bills, not really caring to read any more bad news. She stopped at an envelope Jackie had sent. Why the hell had she mailed the letter when she could've just picked up the phone and called? Jayla tucked the other mail under her arm and used her finger to rip open the envelope, feeling fearful about its contents. She stood there on the curb, reading.

Jaye,

I've lived with something for a very long time. Something I thought I would take to my grave. But the more I learn about you, the more I realize that this is something you need to know, because it could very well be an indication of why you've become the person you are. I'm writing a letter because, honestly, I don't know how we can face each other after this.

That shit hurt like hell when you told me about you and Que. I can't believe you would do that shit to me. But to be honest with you, I think I always suspected something went down between you two. I can only remember the many times Mama tried to talk me out of continuing my relationship with him, saying that he wasn't the man I thought he was. But I ignored all the telltale signs because I refused to believe either of you would betray me like that. But knowing that thought has always lurked in the back of my mind is probably how I have been able to cope with my actions for all these years.

I know what Mama did to you when you were fourteen. I know she gave you misopostrol to induce your labor. I know this because we were in on the plan together. I was pregnant, but I had a miscarriage. I called Mama, crying, because I wanted my baby so bad. I was depressed as hell. She mentioned just adopting yours, because she knew she was going to have to raise that child. You were fourteen and wouldn't know what to do. I was older, more established, nearly engaged to be married, and I would provide a better life for the baby. I was already distraught, and the idea sounded too good to be true.

So, I did my research. I had already had my miscarriage, and it had been a few weeks before, so people were beginning to ask about my baby. I had to hurry and get yours if I wanted to pass her off as my own. I found out you could get some over-the-counter medicine to induce labor. She was supposed to just slip the misopostrol into your drink or food and take you to the hospital, and in your slightly medicated state, you would sign the adoption papers. She would give me the baby to adopt, and no one would be the wiser. That is why you never knew Jasmine was yours. I want you to know no one, not me or Mama, expected you to have a reaction to that medication and slip into a coma. It scared the shit out of us, because they didn't think you would make it. For that, I am terribly sorry.

I don't expect you to understand why I did it. I was hurt. I was in a fucked-up place mentally. And there you were. Single. Fourteen. Pregnant. No job. No man. No money. The shit wasn't fair. I felt I deserved that. Plus, I guess, part of me really thought I was doing you a favor by taking the baby off your hands. You still had your whole life ahead of you. You weren't ready to raise a kid. Mama had tried to convince you to get an abortion, and you'd kept refusing. So, when I lost my baby, it just seemed like it would be a win-win-win for all of us.

No, I don't expect you to forgive me. Hell, I don't even forgive you for sleeping with my man and getting pregnant by him in the first place. With everything that has happened between us, I don't think we can ever get back to a place of love. Maybe Jocelyn was our thread. And since she is gone, what really do we have, Jayla?

I'm not really sure what else to say, other than I'm sorry everything happened the way it did. I'm sorry I had to tell you this way, but I feel you needed to know.

Regards,
Jackie

Tears blotched the paper and smeared the words. Jayla sniffed and reread the letter. Her emotions were so jumbled that she really didn't know how to feel. Anger, yes. She was pissed off. But the hurt she felt seemed to outweigh her rage. It pained her to see just how much hatred she and Jackie had fomented all these years. And the devastating consequences of both their actions pained her as well. Because of them, and especially her, their mother was dead. She couldn't assuage her guilt about that no matter how hard she tried.

Vibrant color pictures caught her eye, and Jayla glanced down to her feet, where a tabloid magazine lay. It had been among the mail she tucked under her arm, and so she must have dropped it while she was reading Jackie's letter. She stooped to pick up the magazine, then glanced at the cover and instantly recognized the pictures splashed across it. The pictures she had given Sheila. The faces of the individuals in the pictures had been blurred to protect their identity, but she clearly recognized theirs positions, that hotel bed, the clothes. But it was the headline on the magazine cover, not the pictures, that had Jayla's eyes ballooning so much that they nearly popped out of her damn face.

PHOTOS LEAKED. SENATOR CAUGHT IN SEXUAL RELATIONSHIP WITH TRANSVESTITE AND IN INCESTUOUS RELATIONSHIP WITH ADULT DAUGHTER.

CHAPTER SEVENTEEN

Jayla

"You have reached the voicemail of Sheila Weston . . ."

Jayla felt her body quivering with anger as she clicked the phone off for the tenth time. So now the bitch wanted to get ghost after she had splashed that bullshit all across the media. Newspapers, magazines, and every damn TV channel that wasn't a children's network. It was everywhere, and that wasn't counting the increasing number of hashtags, tweets, and posts all up and down the social media timeline. She could kill Sheila for going to this extent, for spreading a rumor so degrading about her husband that she had ruined Jayla's life.

Her phone rang, and Jayla snatched it up, praying it was Sheila on the other end. "Hello?"

"Hi. Is this Jayla Morgan?"

Jayla frowned at the unfamiliar woman's voice. "Who is this?"

"This is Melanie Bradshaw with WKTV—"

Jayla clicked the phone off and smacked her teeth. How did the slimy bastards get her number? She was definitely going to have to change that, because it was clear, this was only the beginning of the harassment. Jayla massaged her temples, bracing against the pain of the brewing headache. How the hell was she going to get out of this mess? She was tempted to call Grant but quickly decided against it. He was probably doing his own damage control, not to mention she would need to conjure up some lie about how the pictures were taken in the first place. Damn, she couldn't deal with this right now.

Too anxious to sit, Jayla stood from her bed and began pacing the room as she racked her brain for answers she didn't have. *Her father?* Why the fuck would Sheila make up some crazy-ass rumor like that? It was downright disgusting. There was no way that man could be her father. Sure, she had never known her father, but still. To think she had kissed and sucked the man off was absolutely revolting. They couldn't be related. They just couldn't. That was just Sheila's last-ditch effort to tarnish Grant's image. No, the cheating wasn't enough, and no, the transvestite wasn't enough. She had to dig to the bottom pits of grimy hell to pull some rumor about incest out her ass. The fact that she had even taken it there showed just how sick in the head she was. And the fact that she had dragged Jayla into the limelight with her personal revenge tactics made it all the worse.

Yes, Jayla had been betrayed in her life, and she had done her fair share of betraying. Deception had become so much a part of her lifestyle that she sometimes didn't know where the lie ended and the truth began. But Jayla had held up her end of the bargain with Sheila, and Sheila had played dirty. But they were the rules of the game, nonetheless. Jayla had done nothing to deserve the slander, and the thought of what she would do out of anger chilled her to the bone.

The notification of an incoming text had Jayla's phone vibrating on the bed. She scooped it up and swiped her screen to read the message from Sheila. Just saw the news. We need to talk in person. Meet me at the boat in an hour.

A surge of adrenaline shot through Jayla's body and had her snatching her purse and bolting for the door. This shit was going to end tonight. She was going to demand answers, but regardless of how logical those answers seemed, she knew she was about to beat the brakes off this chick.

As soon as she opened the front door, a swarm of lights flashed in Jayla's face and had her nearly stumbling backward. She squinted, lifting her hand to shield her eyes from the bright lights of cameras, as twenty or so reporters shot rapid-fire questions at her like bullets.

"Ms. Morgan, is it true that Senator Grant Weston is your father?"

"Ms. Morgan, did you know you were sleeping with your dad?"

"Jayla, is it true you're having a baby with the senator?"

"Ms. Morgan, do you have a statement regarding the allegations?"

They were all talking on top of each other, and their voices welded into a jumbled mess. The entire scene was chaotic and grated on her nerves, and she could feel her temper reigniting. Jayla parted her lips, and as if she had flipped a switch, the crowd hushed, and multiple microphones were shoved in her face.

"First off," she snapped, her eyes sharpened like daggers as she glared at the cameras in her face, "I don't give a fuck what anybody told y'all, but Grant Weston is not my damn father."

"Ms. Morgan, who is your father?" asked a brunette reporter in the front as she scribbled notes on her pad.

"It doesn't fucking matter. It's not Grant."

"Ms. Morgan, is that you in the photos?" This time, a pudgy reporter with glasses shoved the microphone so damn close to Jayla's face, he nearly busted her lip.

Jayla felt a fresh wave of anger rising. In addition to the pictures she had taken, there were pictures of her circulating that she'd had no idea would be used this way. The bitch. "Yeah," she murmured, then immediately cursed herself for admitting this. These leeches were going to take that shit and run with it.

"So, you were having an affair with the very married Senator Grant Weston?" the pudgy reporter asked.

Jayla pursed her lips and shook her head, then stepped off the porch and shoved through the crowd. She had already run her big mouth too much, and she just needed to get away from these media vultures before her words were all twisted up. They called her name and fired off more questions, but she just tuned them out and held her palm up in front of one of the cameras to prevent the lens from catching any more of the embarrassing scene.

TV station vans cluttered her driveway to the point where she was blocked in. She turned around, and again, everyone fell silent in order to record what she had to say. "Y'all better get off my property, before I set all this shit on fire out here. Bounce. We're done." When a few of the reporters moved their vehicles just enough to allow her to make an exit, Jayla jumped in her car and sped down the driveway. She turned onto the road and hit the accelerator.

Guilt and embarrassment had her mind out of focus to such a degree that she didn't even realize she was pushing eighty miles an hour until she skidded against a curb and barely missed hitting an oncoming vehicle. She braked and came to a stop on the side of the road. Realizing her emotions had gotten the best of her, she took a deep breath to calm her nerves. *Get a grip*, she scolded herself as her heart thudded against her rib cage.

Once she felt calmer, she eased back onto the road and kept her mind on the task at hand. She needed to get to Sheila so they could sort this mess out. Attention was something she was used to, given her line of work, but she definitely wasn't used to this kind of public scrutiny. It was disturbing and somewhat scary to have that many people in her business. She feared that she would never have any privacy again. Plus, she couldn't stand being the subject of such a disgusting story. People thought it was that gross that she would spread her legs for her own blood relative. Not just any relative, but her own father. The media had pounced on the allegation and treated it as gospel, and she knew whatever the outcome of this whole ordeal, she would never have peace again.

Jayla pulled up to the dock and parked her car, and then she hurried down the wooden planks as the ocean air slapped her cheeks. *Empress Weston* was sitting in the same slip as before, bobbing lightly in the wind, little waves splashing against the bow. Sheila was perched on the aft deck of the boat. Her hands grasped the railing as she leaned over and looked out to sea. To Jayla's surprise, Sheila wasn't dressed like she had just stepped off a runway today. Instead, she was casual in a button-up blue-jean dress that stopped at her knees, a brown waist belt, and brown flats. Jayla hadn't thought either one of the Westons even knew what "jean" material looked like, much less owned an article of denim clothing.

Jayla stepped aboard, her fists clenched. She was itching to bust a bitch now and ask questions later, but she restrained herself when she noticed that Sheila looked . . . off. Whether she was distraught or anxious or calculating her next conniving move, the difference in her aura was unmistakable. And for once, she wasn't sucking one of those damn cigarettes.

Hearing Jayla approach, Sheila turned. "I figured you would've run to the media with this shit." Her tone was cool, and a hint of anger was clearly beneath the surface.

Jayla frowned. "Me? Run to the media? What the fuck are you talking about?"

"I saw your little interview, Jayla."

"Those idiots were all over at my house, sticking cameras in my face and spitting lies about me. What was I supposed to do?" When Sheila just shook her head, Jayla barreled on. "And you've got some fucking nerve coming at me! You knew what you were doing when your ass leaked those pictures to the press."

Sheila grinned as she shook her head. "No, you don't understand."

"Oh, I don't?" Jayla stepped to Sheila's face now, forcing their noses to brush. "This is what you've been planning all along. I knew I couldn't trust your snake ass. Got me gathering all this shit for you because you're claiming you want to bring Grant down. What the hell did you have against me to start those sick-ass rumors, Sheila? I could just drag your ass all up and down this raggedy-ass deck for that shit."

Sheila didn't falter, and her voice remained calm as she shook her head again. "You swear you know everything, but you don't know shit. How the hell did I know that Grant is your father? I didn't even know you before I met you. Had never heard of you before in my life."

"He is *not* my father! And you're right you didn't know me any more than I knew you, and that's why you made that up. My question is, why? What the fuck did you have to gain from that?"

"Exactly." Sheila's eyes narrowed, as if to indicate that Jayla had answered her own question. "What the fuck did I gain from that? Absolutely nothing. And you should know me by now to know that I'm greedy and selfish. I like power. I like money. I like sex. But if it don't benefit me, then it's a waste of my damn time."

Jayla stepped back, shaking her own head, as she struggled to make sense of the situation. "So, where the hell did they get that? You're the one that leaked the pictures, so they had to get it from you, or are you telling me they just made up the rumor about Grant being my father?"

"That's just it," Sheila said. "I don't know where they got it from, because I'm not the one who leaked those pictures."

Jayla rolled her eyes. "Oh yeah, whatever. That's what you wanted the proof for. That's what you begged me to get you, so you could embarrass Grant, remember? Or have we forgotten our little deal?"

"I know. And I had every intention of doing so." Sheila made her way up to the cockpit, Jayla right on her heels, and pulled the envelope with the photos from a drawer and placed it on a bench seat. "When *I* was ready. I told you I like power. I was going to use these to blackmail Grant for a little bit. See what I could squeeze out of him first. Then I was going to the media. I didn't leak those photos, Jayla. And I damn sure didn't spread that rumor about you being Grant's daughter. Now, believe what you want, but I'm telling the truth."

Sheila's words struck Jayla like a gut punch, rendering her speechless. That wasn't possible. If Sheila didn't leak those pictures, who did? And why? Jayla's mind immediately flashed to Carl. He was the only other person who had had access to that camera. But he hadn't wanted to go through with the plan. Why would he have released the pictures and risked slandering himself in the process? Unless someone paid him so much for the information that the dollar figure trumped his reputation. When money was involved, people would do anything.

Jayla pulled out her phone and smacked her lips at the shaded gray bars on the screen, which indicated she had no reception out here. She looked back up and watched as Sheila pulled out her cigarettes. "You seem real calm about this whole situation," Jayla noted with a suspicious frown. "Is there something else you're not telling me?"

A flame danced across Sheila's face as she lit her cigarette. "Like what?" she asked coolly.

"For starters, what are you trying to get out of all of this?"

Sheila sighed, and for once, it seemed like her face softened. "I married Grant as a means to come up," she explained. "I didn't love him. He didn't love me. But I was pretty, I was smart, and he needed me as a trophy wife. Someone to smile beside him in public and get their hands dirty for him in private. Having grown up on welfare, I jumped at the opportunity. I was younger than him, but I didn't care so much about him as I did a comfortable lifestyle. I always wanted to get married, have kids, and have money, and he seemed to be the one to give me all three."

Sheila paused and flicked the cigarette over the side of the boat and into the water. Her forehead had creased with anger as she began to relive her words in her mind. "So, this thing, this marriage we had, worked for us. I did the illegal shit I had to do to push him up the political chain. You name it, I did it. Bribes, sexing for votes, whatever it took to make sure he was a success. And in exchange, I knew I would be set. Until he started sleeping around.

"At first, I ignored it, because it wasn't that big of a deal to me. I had the title, and I was the one with all the benefits. But then he started pulling back and putting me on restrictions. Giving me spending limits and allowances and wanting to pay the bills himself so he could monitor the money. Strike one. Then he starts talking in his sleep and hanging out with this one particular chick who is too damn young for his old ass, but she done got it in his head that they're in love, and he's claiming he's going to leave me for her."

Sheila's eyes were fully ablaze now from the heat of her statement. "Oh, I don't think so, not when I'm the one that's been with him from the beginning. Not when I'm the one that has been doing everything to get him where he is. I fucking *made* that nigga. He can't even take a shit by himself, because he would need me to show him how to wipe his raggedy ass. And he has the nerve to tell me he's leaving me? Wrong. Strike two."

Jayla watched her pace the cockpit so much, it was a wonder she didn't break through the decking. Shock at the whole story had her shaking her head. "So, what was strike three?"

Sheila stopped pacing. Her entire body seemed to deflate, as if the severity of her impending words had weakened her. "I went to the doctor," she murmured. "I had been having symptoms, and I just knew I was pregnant. I was so excited because I had been trying to have Grant's baby. I've always wanted to be a mother. Grant had Marcus, but he wasn't my kid. I didn't like him, and he didn't like me."

Jayla remembered Sheila's sentiment about the death of her stepson. The final piece of the puzzle.

"So, like I said, I thought I was pregnant. Had even gone out to buy little baby items and everything. Started making a list of names. I just knew Grant was going to be so happy when I told him, but I wanted to wait to get confirmation from the doctor. I get there, and they tell me that I'm not pregnant, and that I'm actually in premature menopause. Imagine my surprise. I'm only forty. I wasn't going to think about menopause for at least another ten years."

"Yeah, but really, Sheila, your age had something to do with you not being able to get pregnant. No offense, but it's not like you're in your twenties."

Sheila smirked. "True," she said with a nod. "But I think the HIV Grant gave me had something to do with it as well."

Jayla gasped as Sheila held up three fingers and wiggled them back and forth. *Strike three.* Then Jayla remembered something Sheila had said, and her eyes widened with the realization. "So that young woman at the funeral . . . Jasmine. Is that her?"

"Yeah," Sheila answered. "That's the bitch."

Sheila had mentioned that she didn't know who Jasmine was. Now, with the ties that bound them, Jayla could easily see why she had lied. Why wasn't she surprised? Jasmine was up to her same old tricks, and Jayla wondered just how deep she was in her latest web of deception.

"How do you know her?" Sheila asked all of a sudden.

Jayla turned up her lips in disgust. She started to respond but stopped short when she saw Sheila was no longer paying attention to her. She turned to see an image of Grant on the flat-screen TV mounted behind the bar in the cockpit. He looked disheveled as he stood at a podium, flashing cameras illuminating the troubled look on his face. With those dark circles around his sunken eyes and deep wrinkles across his forehead and around his mouth, he looked like he had aged fifty-plus years in a matter of hours. Sheila reached for the remote control and stabbed the volume button to turn up the sound.

"I can honestly say that I did not create or assist in the dissemination of the video or the pictures," Grant was saying, his voice laced with embarrassment. He gripped the sides of the podium so hard, his knuckles were sheet white. "As your senator, I want to say to each of you simply and directly that I am deeply sorry for my irresponsible and selfish behavior. The issue at hand is not my engagement in the sexual act depicted in the photos. The issue is my failure to uphold the standards as a public figure and the representative of my people. I have disappointed you all, and for that, I am more ashamed. My behavior was irresponsible, unacceptable, and I solely accept all responsibility for my actions. I would also like to extend my deepest apology to the other parties involved and featured in the video and pictures. This information is very damaging to their credibility and their character, and I humbly request that they are not harassed or slandered in any way as a result of my personal indiscretions."

When he lowered his eyes, Jayla could've sworn she saw the slight gleam of a tear at the corner of his right eye. She couldn't deny the tug on her heart. He looked so broken. All because he was a man of power and had been used as a pawn in some financial and power struggle between Jasmine and Sheila. It was disheartening to watch the effects of all the selfishness and deceit.

"Furthermore," Grant continued, his voice cracking, "given the sensitivity of this issue, I am stepping down from my position as senator. I had hoped to be able to continue the work that the citizens of this state elected me to do, but unfortunately, the distraction that I have created has made that impossible. My resignation is effective immediately, and so it is incumbent on my colleagues to return to work immediately, so that the people can select a new senator and, most importantly, so that my wife and I can heal from the damage that I have caused."

Sheila laughed, clearly amused by his last line. "Yeah, right, asshole," she muttered. "I did not once hear your apology to me for your bullshit."

Jayla sighed and shook her head at how everything had come to pass. It was just too much. "So now what?" she asked.

"Don't worry," Sheila said. "I'll handle it." It was clear there was more to be said, but Sheila kept her mouth shut as her eyes narrowed in concentration.

CHAPTER EIGHTEEN

Jayla

The muffled ringtone of her cell phone broke the air, and Jayla absently shoved her hand in her purse, fumbled over her wallet and balled-up receipts in search of the mini device. One day she would clean out the mess that was her purse. Halfway distracted, she didn't notice the squad car until she'd crossed the parking lot and reached the doors of the store. The squad car's red and blue lights spilled across the concrete like liquid and pulled Jayla's eyes from her purse to the pavement, up to the crisp white bumper, and then to the police officer leaning comfortably against the hood. Her hand paused in mid-search, and she tuned out the phone's ringing as she pretended not to notice that the short sleeves of the officer's burgundy button-up revealed toned arms, which were now crossed over his chest. Pretended not to notice the way his muscles flexed as he let his arms fall to his sides while he unfolded himself from his position in much the way one would perform a lazy stretch. Damn, he was sexy, she mused, as the hint of a smile tugged at his lips as his eyes held hers.

The officer had been in such a hurry, he hadn't even bothered to park but had merely pulled parallel to the building, blocking in two cars in the process. The dull hum of the squad's car engine hung between them, and then came the sound of his even footsteps as he started toward her.

"Jayla Morgan?" he asked, though it was obvious he already knew her identity.

Jayla frowned. "Do I know you?"

"Not yet." He smiled, attempting to thaw her suspicion. "Officer Davis. Why don't you come with me for a few minutes?"

Shit. He was the officer who had left her phone messages. Jayla's eyes narrowed a fraction as she sidestepped him. Suddenly, his ass didn't seem so sexy anymore. "Not interested," she said.

His hand lifted to her stomach to stop her from walking by him. The touch was gentle but firm enough to show that his question wasn't a suggestion but more of a demand. She didn't know why his hand on her sent a charge piercing through her body, but she ignored the feeling and stepped back to break the contact.

"I'm not interested," she repeated more forcefully.

"I understand that," he said. "But you see, we received a tip a while back, and we want to question you regarding the circumstances of your mother's death."

Jayla kept her face stoic to hide her apprehension. She rolled her eyes. "My mother?"

"Jillian Morgan? That is your mother, right?"

"Since you've got all the answers, why are you bothering me?" Jayla snapped and took a step to walk past him.

Just as fast, Officer Davis stepped in her path. "You see, that's the thing. I don't have all the answers. That's why I need to talk to you."

"I don't know anything, Officer," Jayla told him, struggling to keep the desperation out of her voice. "I really don't. As if you haven't heard, I'm in the middle of a scandal with Senator Weston. And a good friend of mine just died, and I'm trying to get my life together. Please just leave me alone."

Officer Davis gestured toward his car. "Then you won't mind answering a few questions for me." His tone was a little more forceful now, as he had grown impatient. "It'll be quick. Then I'll have my boys bring you right back here so you can finish your day. The quicker we can get this handled, the quicker we can close out this issue and relieve you of being a person of interest in this investigation."

Jayla didn't move, still conflicted about her options. At the same time, she was scared, but she didn't know if refusing to comply would come back to bite her. Or if her avoidance of the police made her look even more guilty. So, it was probably better to get this over with, and hopefully, she could spin a tale convincing enough to get off the cops' radar.

"Fine," she agreed.

They rode in heavy silence. Sitting in the back of the police car, a grid of metal bars separating her from the front of the squad car, Jayla couldn't help feeling increasing anxiety as Officer Davis drove her downtown. She focused on the details of that night and what she would tell the police. Her story from their initial investigation all those years ago replayed in her head. She didn't know anything, she'd said back then. She had just had her baby and had come out of a coma, for God's sake! She had locked herself in her bedroom, crying and sleeping off the pain.

The coroner had found painkillers in Jillian's system, but the detectives hadn't been able to prove Jayla had given them to her. Her mother had gotten Jayla's prescription filled, so the police had had no way of knowing if Jayla had given her the pills or if she had administered them to herself, unaware of their adverse effect when coupled with her alcohol. It was simple and believable argument. So why was she shitting bricks on the tattered leather seat of the cop car? She knew the answer. *Quentin.* In her grief, she had spilled everything to Quentin, and she didn't know if he had approached the police and pointed a finger in her direction. That shit was killing her. Even worse, how much more would he divulge to the police if he didn't get his way?

"Tell me a little about yourself, Jayla Morgan," Officer Davis said, meeting her eyes in the rearview mirror. He was grinning, clearly feeling triumphant with this turn of events.

"For what reason?" Jayla retorted, not even bothering to mask her irritation. "For you to use against me in a court of law? That's how y'all do it, right?"

He chuckled. "I can see how you would think that. But I'm being serious, and this is strictly off the record. Not business related."

"So, personal?"

He shrugged. "I guess you could say that." He grinned at her in the rearview mirror.

His smile was genuine, she decided, and to her shock, it diffused her annoyance with the situation. To a small degree anyway. He kept glancing at her in the rearview mirror. She couldn't figure out why, but it was making her uncomfortable, so she focused her eyes on the window. "You should really keep business and pleasure separate, Officer Davis," she murmured.

"You're right," he agreed. "But there is something about you, Ms. Morgan. What is it?"

In any other circumstance, Jayla would've taken that opportunity and run with it. The man was fine, but that was not her problem right now. So instead of entertaining the open invitation to flirt, Jayla remained quiet.

"Okay." Officer Davis nodded. "How about I tell you a little bit about myself? Just to show good faith?" He didn't pause for a response. "I'm Kelton Davis. I'm thirty-four years old. I've been a cop for six years. I'm divorced, and I have custody of my two-year-old son, Nicholas. Let's see. I love—"

"Kelton," Jayla said, jumping in, "I don't mean to interrupt, but I really am not trying to get to know you. This is really not the place, and now is not the time."

"I must say, for a politician's daughter, you are not a real people person, are you?"

"Excuse me?" Jayla's anger simmered at the offhand statement. "That nigga is not my father. Don't believe everything you hear."

Clearly taken aback and confused by her outburst, Kelton drew his eyebrows together. "I apologize. I didn't mean to offend you," he said. "I thought—"

"Wrong," Jayla snapped, interrupting him again. "You thought wrong. Grant is not my dad, so if you're looking to grill me on some exclusive-type shit to go run your mouth about, you can swallow it right now." She hadn't really meant to go off, but dammit, her nerves were shot to hell, and she was tired of the scrutiny. She couldn't wait to get this over with.

At that very moment, she felt her phone vibrate from an incoming text. Jayla pulled it out and read the message from Sheila. We need to talk ASAP. Call me. Finally got in touch with Carl. Jayla wondered what they needed to talk about, but even more so, she wanted to know how Sheila was able to get in touch with Carl. He had conveniently been avoiding Jayla since the night at the hotel. Jayla had started to text back when she saw that Kelton was wheeling the car into the police department's parking lot. Sheila would have to wait. One issue at a time.

The door slamming had Jayla snatching her eyes open. She hadn't realized she'd dozed off. With a groan, she lifted her head from the table and turned her eyes to the door. She was shocked to see Heather standing there, a pin-striped suit and a blue silk blouse accenting her trim figure. The woman had chopped her blond hair into a cute bob that flirted with her chin, and her previously pale white skin had a tan tint to it, a sign that she had spent quite a few days in the sun. Jayla didn't remember her wearing glasses before, but she had a pair of thin wire frames perched on her face. Jayla's shock wore off and was replaced by anger. This bitch had some nerve.

"Rested?" Heather asked as she moseyed toward Jayla at the table.

Jayla glanced around and was not surprised when she didn't see a clock on any of the four walls of the interrogation room. "How long have I been here?" she asked. Sleep still coated her voice.

"Not long enough," Heather responded with a smirk. She sat a paper cup on the table and took a seat across from her. Grateful, Jayla took a sip of the lukewarm water. She cringed. It tasted like pond water, but it was still a refreshing relief, nonetheless. It felt like she had been cooped up in that tiny room for days. She took another tender sip.

"Well, it is a pleasure to see you again, Jayla," Heather began, clasping her fingers together on the table.

"I wish I could say the same."

"Oh, come on now." Heather feigned a pout. "Don't be like that. You know we have history. Me, you, and Reggie."

The thought of the whole ordeal had a stream of curses simmering on Jayla's tongue. Heather had been an assignment, or so she had thought. She had actually been setting up a sting operation to get Jayla arrested. And Reggie . . . Well, Reggie had found out that Heather was setting him up, and he had taken advantage of Jayla in the strip club. She had even been raped that night. Jayla took another sip of water, wondering how she could drown this white bitch with what she had left in the cup.

"So, have you had a chance to reflect on the situation?" Heather asked.

"I don't even know what situation you're referring to," Jayla said, irritated. "You drag me in here . . . I don't know . . . how long ago. You won't even let me out to sleep, shit, or shower. I just have to sit here while y'all stare at me on the other side of that damn two-way glass. I was told I was being brought down here for a couple of questions. I'm sure y'all have violated some kind of rights."

Heather chuckled. "I assure you, Jayla," she said, her lips curved in amusement, "we have not violated any of your rights. You have been brought down for questioning. But as I'm sure you know, we're very busy here at the precinct. But I can understand your . . . impatience. What with your line of work, you're anxious to turn your next trick, right?"

Smart bitch, Jayla thought with a roll of her eye.

"You're not in that line of work still, are you, Jayla?" Heather asked, pressing.

Jayla smacked her teeth. “Can you just ask me what you need to ask me, so I can go?” she snapped.

“Sure. Tell me about your mother, Jillian Morgan.”

“She’s dead. What the hell do you want me to say that you don’t already know?”

Heather nodded, unfazed. “That’s right. So next, why don’t you tell me how you killed her?”

Jayla’s eyes ballooned with shock. “Excuse me?”

“Oh, come on.” Heather’s voice remained calm. She was clearly enjoying toying with her. “You know we wouldn’t have pulled you in here on a hunch. You must know we have some hard evidence. And it’s all pointing at you.” She pointed her finger at Jayla for effect.

“Why don’t you just arrest me, then?” Jayla responded boldly.

“Well, I don’t know. Maybe I’m like you, and I just like fucking around with people.”

Jayla shut her eyes and slowly counted to ten. She didn’t want to slam a police officer up against the wall. She really didn’t want to go back to jail. But Heather was good. She knew what she was doing.

Heather unfolded herself from her seat and leaned into Jayla’s face. Her nose nearly touched Jayla’s. “Listen, you little bitch,” she whispered, the stench of Chinese food beating Jayla in the face. “I don’t have time for your games. I’ve thrown you in jail once. I can do it again. So, you don't want to fuck with me. Tell me the truth and maybe we can work out a plea deal. You won't even spend that long in jail."

Jayla didn't break her stare. She would not let this bitch weaken her again. "I don't know what you're talking about," she replied through tight lips.

"I know you did it," Heather said. "That anonymous tip gave me just enough to know it was you. Five minutes with that person and I'll have everything I need to throw you into jail. Until then, you're free to go, but I suggest you stay close and practice how you're going to pick up the soap." She gave a smile before heading to the door.

Jayla's breath came out in a gush of air when Heather left the room. She felt like she was being suffocated. She stood and left the room herself, then walked numbly down a long hallway until she reached the entrance to the station and pushed through the door.

It was night. So, she had been in there for many hours, just like she had figured. Jayla inhaled the cool air and fell to her knees on the sidewalk, letting the tears fall. It never failed. She had been hit with so much karma that it was a wonder she was still in her right mind. She rose to her feet, shaking her head fiercely, and was just about to start walking when her peripheral caught a man coming toward her.

Jayla wanted to struggle but couldn't resist when his arms encircled her. Her knees gave way again, and she would've collapsed once more had he not held her against him. She surrendered, just let the tears trail lazily down her cheeks to dampen his shirt. Damn, it felt good to be held. Why did it feel so right to be in his arms? His cheek rested on her forehead, and she lifted her face, eyed him through the tears glittering on her lashes. "Derrick," she whispered.

"Jayla."

She blinked as the man's features came into focus. A short crop of slick, curly hair, honey complexion, hazel eyes. No, not Derrick. Kelton. Kelton, the police officer. What the hell was she doing? Jayla snatched back as if she had been stung, and hugged herself with a sigh.

"I'm sorry," she murmured, swallowing the initial bout of embarrassment. "I just . . . I don't know what's wrong with me." She laughed, but her laugh was way too forced for either of them to believe it. She sniffed and swiped at her tears with the sleeve of her shirt.

"I was looking for you," Kelton said. "I wanted to give you a ride back. You okay?"

"What difference does it make to you?" she murmured. "I'm just another suspect in your investigation."

"Hey, what's wrong?"

She ignored his genuine concern. If she paid it any mind, she would be reminded again about how pathetic her life was. "Just leave me alone, Kelton. I'll just take a cab or something."

"Listen." He surprised both of them when he rested his palm on her cheek. His eyes reflected the sincerity that dripped from his words when he said, "I don't know you at all, but you look like you could use an ear. Let me take you to get something to eat."

Jayla was already shaking her head. "No. For what? For you to twist my words for your investigation? I don't trust you."

He dropped his head and nodded. "I know. Well, at least let me take you back to your car, Jayla. It's late."

Jayla pulled away from his hand on her face and stood up straighter. "Fine," she said. "Take me to my car. I don't feel like talking. I don't feel like being bothered. All right?"

Kelton nodded and reached out to guide her with his hand, but he stopped when she pulled away from him again. He led the way back to his car and opened his passenger door for her. She climbed in, still not saying a word.

The ride back was more tense than before. Jayla rested her head on the headrest and watched the buildings whizz by. A part of her wished Kelton had been completely serious. That he didn't have ulterior motives. She could use someone in her face that wasn't busy trying to figure out how to stick a knife in her back. But right now, she didn't feel up to mingling. She was more in the mood for solitude. A long bath mixed with essential oils, maybe a glass of wine to mellow out and take her mind off everything. Perhaps she could find something that hadn't expired somewhere among the frozen dinner boxes stuffed in her freezer.

She tried not to linger too long on Kelton's delicious cologne, which had the smell of peppermint filling the Chrysler. Or the few times he would glance her way. It was really uncomfortable, but Jayla had to admit, she hadn't had any genuine male interest since Derrick. The attention felt a little nice. Maybe if the timing wasn't so inopportune. And maybe if he wasn't a damn cop.

Jayla was surprised when he turned into the entrance to a McDonald's. She peered through the windshield, watching him steer the car to the drive-through. The thought of food had her stomach rumbling. She couldn't remember the last time she had eaten.

"You want a burger or something?" Kelton asked absently.

Jayla smirked. "Real slick."

"What? I'm starving, and it would be rude of me to get something for myself without asking you."

Jayla watched his grin spread, and she masked her own smile with a frown. He was doing his utmost to get her to loosen up. It was cute.

They ordered their food, and as soon as the cashier handed over two bags and two cups, Kelton eased the car into a parking space.

"This is not a date or anything," Jayla said as she opened her bag. She had relaxed a little, and the smell of grease was making her mouth water. She popped a few fries in her mouth and licked the salt from her fingers.

"I know," he said. "We're just two sexy folks sharing a meal and *not* trying to get to know each other."

"Exactly."

The sound of their eating filled the car, and Jayla felt lulled in the comfortable silence. Kelton didn't know it, but him inviting her to share a meal made her feel a little easier about her case. He didn't seem like the type of person to eat dinner with someone he thought had murdered her own mother. So, all that bullshit Heather had tried to get her hyped about at the precinct was just that, bullshit. But Heather had done a great job of instilling fear in Jayla, that was for sure.

She tossed a sideways glance at Kelton and noticed he was watching her intently. She slipped her straw between her lips and sucked the sweet tea from the cup.

"What is it?" she asked finally, as Kelton continued to stare. "I got food on my face or something?"

He shook his head. "No. You're just so beautiful."

"Yeah, yeah." Jayla rolled her eyes at the compliment. "I've gotten that one before. Is that all you see? A beautiful face and a sexy-ass body?"

"No. I see a woman who is weighed down by a whole lot of shit in life. You look like you've had it hard."

Jayla put on a plastic smile to cover her reaction to his accurate assessment. "What do you know about a hard life, Officer Davis?" She tried to keep the acid out of her voice. "You look like you come from money. I can almost smell it on you. You had both parents, right? Only child? Private school and captain of your school's lacrosse or water polo team? Full scholarship to undergrad and grad school? Let me know when none of what I say applies." Jayla didn't know if she had struck a chord, but she saw a flicker of sadness in his eyes before he blinked it away.

"Close," he said. "Mother died while giving birth to me. I was raised by a single father, who beat me and raped my baby sister every chance he got. I pressed charges, but I was just a teenager, and nothing would stick. He never went to jail. He was murdered by some prostitute who was trying to rob him. I put myself and my sister through school and swore I'd become a cop to put away bastards like him."

Jayla eyed him, in shock. She never would've known by observing him. It just proved how much you could look at someone and not know their struggle. Hell, she was living proof of that herself. "What happened to your sister?" she asked.

The question brought a proud light to his face, and Kelton grinned. "Great. She just graduated from medical school and is doing her residency in Chicago."

Jayla smiled. It felt good to hear some kind of happy ending. "You said you have kids?"

"One kid. Nicholas. He is in that terrible-two thing, but that's my little man. I had a daughter . . ." He trailed off and sighed as the memory tugged on his heart. "Nick's mother, Deidre . . . We're not technically together, but we did sleep together a few times. This last time, she got pregnant. She had my daughter a few weeks ago, but my baby died in the hospital nursery. When the nurse, Karmen or Kimora or someone, came in to tell us, Deidre requested to see the baby. She hasn't been the same since. I've got full custody of Nick, because she damn near went crazy. She doesn't even want to play any part in her son's life now."

"Damn," Jayla murmured, with a shake of her head. "That must have been rough."

"Very. But I'm just being strong for my son." He blew out a breath and took a sip of his Coke. "Now your turn," he said with a fresh smile. "What is your hard life story, Jayla Morgan?"

Jayla lowered her eyes. No way she would tell this man everything she had done, everything that had been done to her. But she did tell him what had been playing in the recesses of her mind for the longest time and pained her even to utter the words.

"I'm dying," she murmured. "I have HIV."

For what seemed like hours, Kelton didn't say anything. Jayla was afraid to look at him and see that familiar expression of disgust and judgment. She was tainted. She was dirty. Soiled. She had been a ho and had to live forever with the evidence of that.

Kelton's skin was warm on hers as he took her hand and hesitantly lifted it to his face. Jayla watched in stunned silence as he kissed each of her knuckles one by one, his thick lips caressing her skin like silk. "You're beautiful," he whispered. "And you need to be strong. I don't know your story, Jayla Morgan. I don't know your past. But you look like you've given up on your future."

I have, Jayla thought. She had given up on happiness and a "real" life. Shit like that seemed like a fairy tale to people like her. But she held on to his hope. It seemed strong enough for both of them at the moment.

After they finished their meal, Kelton pulled out of the McDonald's parking lot and onto the road. They had gotten back to Jayla's side of town when she spotted a group of nighttime partygoers in the lights cast by a large building. Then Jayla saw her. Well, not her, *them*. She leaned into the window, sure she wasn't seeing what she thought she was seeing. But she was.

"Stop the car!" she yelled, already fumbling for the door handle.

"What?"

"Stop the car, Kelton. Now!"

Obediently, he wheeled the car to the curb and hit the brakes. Jayla jumped out and did not even bother to close the door. She took off running down the sidewalk, determined to catch up with them, with her. Now they stood together in a parking lot. As Jayla closed the distance, she knew for sure it was her. She just knew it. The clothes, the hair . . . How could she forget? But the question was, what the hell was going on? Anger had her chest tightening, but she didn't stop as she rounded the corner.

The two of them were engaged in such a deep conversation that they didn't even notice her running toward them, so when she reached them, her presence startled them both. Jayla opened her mouth, struggling to catch her breath. Her eyes narrowed to Sheila first. She knew this bitch couldn't be trusted. She knew that from the moment she first laid eyes on her. But never in a million years had she thought . . .

"Well, well, nice to see you too, Puma," Patricia said, with an amused smirk.

CHAPTER NINETEEN

Jayla

"What the fuck is going on here?" Jayla all but screamed as she watched Patricia's smug expression. The last time she saw the woman, she had looked so frail, not to mention bald. Now she sported an expensive pantsuit, had that familiar glow to her skin, and was quite a few pounds heavier than she was when she "died." She had on a different wig, and it was styled in a cute updo, with curls falling to brush her cheeks. Her makeup and expensive jewelry were perfect. While watching Patricia "waste away" had been one fucked-up nightmare, the fact was that it had never even happened.

Jayla shook her head. She had seen it all. "You're supposed to be dead," she barked, pointing at Patricia. She turned her finger on Sheila. "And you . . . I knew you were a fucking liar when you were giving me all that bullshit on the boat."

Sheila puffed on her cigarette, the wind whipping her hair in her face, as she glanced around at the people passing by. "We probably should continue this somewhere in private," she said.

"No! Fuck that. Patricia, why aren't you dead?"

"Is everything okay?" said a male voice.

Jayla cursed under her breath and turned around to meet Kelton's concerned gaze. His eyes flickered between the ladies, and she could've sworn she heard Sheila and Patricia snicker.

"Everything is fine," Jayla lied through clenched teeth. "Just talking with some *friends*." And because he didn't move an inch after she said that, she took his arm and guided him to the curb. "Can you just wait in the car for me please? I'll only be a second."

Kelton nodded and headed back to his parking space about thirty feet down the street.

Satisfied that Kelton was out of earshot, Jayla stalked back over to the pair of women, whose eyes seemed to be glinting at the unexpected visitor.

"Explain," Jayla demanded. "Now."

Patricia stepped a few feet away and lowered herself onto a bench near the sidewalk. Jayla and Sheila inched over to the bench. "Sit down, Puma." Patricia continued when Jayla made no move to comply. "I needed to fake my death," she admitted, her tone hushed. "Things had gotten out of control, and I had to make a way for me to get out of the situation."

As she spoke, images of lottery tickets and casino receipts flashed in Jayla's head. "You have a gambling problem," she said for Patricia.

Patricia waved her hand, as if to dismiss the idea. "That's what they say," she said with a shrug. "I saw it different. I saw it as an investment. But either way, I won a lot, and I lost even more. Eventually, I started borrowing from some really crazy-ass folks, and when I couldn't pay it back, I knew I had to do something."

"You don't have cancer? How do you fake cancer, Patricia? I saw you losing weight. Your hair. You—"

"Dear, it's really not as hard as it seems," Patricia answered, cutting Jayla off. "Some medication and skipped meals, a razor and a hella of a theater performance. And, of course, a few doctors in your pocket to confirm the news of my death really ices the cake. Don't you think?"

But . . ." Jayla shook her head, struggling to make sense of this confession. This couldn't be real. But Patricia seemed so proud of herself. "Patricia, why didn't you just tell me? Why did you have to make me think you were dead? I cried for you! I thought . . ." Jayla caught a glimpse of Sheila out of her peripheral, and she turned to her. "You had her cremated, you said. You knew about this the whole time? You were in on it with her?"

"Some of it," Sheila said. "But Patricia deceived me too. When I found out about the pictures, I knew she had done that snake shit. I knew there was no way Carl had done it and risked exposing himself."

Patricia leaked the photos? How? Why? Jayla fixed her eyes back on the woman she had loved and trusted all those years. But that woman was gone now. This deceptive snake that sat on the bench like she hadn't done a damn thing wasn't her Patricia. No way she had been played for so long.

"Go ahead, Patricia," Sheila said. "Explain it to her like you explained it to me."

Patricia sighed. "Fine. Damn," she huffed. "Yes, okay, I lied, Puma. I set the whole thing up. Me and Sheila have known each other for damn near forever, so when she approached me to help her with Grant, I figured this was a way to get even. Not just on her, but on you too, Jayla."

"Me?" Jayla choked out the word. "*Me*? Why me? What have I ever done to you?"

Patricia studied her face. "Damn! You look just like that ugly bitch," she murmured in disgust.

Jayla opened her mouth to ask who, but then it struck her like lightning. "My mother?" she whispered. "You've got some kind of personal shit against my mother?"

When Patricia remained quiet, Sheila spoke up. "Go ahead, Patricia. Tell her how you've hated her for her mother since you met her. Tell her how you sought her out for your sick little revenge."

Jayla's heart felt like it burst into a million pieces. It couldn't be true. It just couldn't. All this time?

"Grant and I were a couple a long time ago," Patricia said, her voice nonchalant. Apparently, whatever she was about to say didn't touch her one bit. "I mean, I loved that man something awful. Gave him my heart and soul. This was before I got into the appraising business, of course. Do you know this man had the nerve to cheat on me with Jillian? Grant had never cheated on me until that bitch started throwing her panties in his face. So, what did he do? He took the bait and started sleeping with her."

Jayla gritted her teeth. The fact that this woman was speaking about her deceased mother in such a derogatory manner left a feeling of nausea in the pit of her stomach.

"So, lo and behold, Jillian turns up pregnant," Patricia continued. "She's all in Grant's ear about them being together and raising their baby together. Mind you she already had a child—your sister Jackie—by some other guy, who had gone to prison, so I know the bitch didn't love Grant. She just wanted somebody to help her raise her kids." She shrugged again. "Or she may have loved him. I don't know. But it didn't matter. I was Grant's woman. She was just a side piece that I *allowed* Grant to play around with from time to time.

Grant started eating into her mess, and he starts talking about how he needed to be a better man, settle down with Jillian since she was the mother of his daughter, and how she would make a great politician's wife. I'm mad because I loved Grant with my everything, and he was supposed to propose to me. But he had actually fallen in love with Jillian! And he was going to leave me for her. I knew the bitch had to go. So, the moment you were born, Grant wants to rush all up to the hospital, because he swears you're his. And I couldn't have that. So, I paid a nurse to switch the paternity tests."

Jayla squeezed her eyes shut, as if to deny the truth. Patricia had delivered this news just as casually as if she had said she switched meals on the dinner menu or dresses for a party. What type of sick individual went and switched paternity tests to keep a woman away from her man?

Then Patricia's words finally sank in, as if they had been slowly branded on Jayla's brain. If she switched paternity tests, then that meant . . .

"Yes, Puma," Patricia said, verbalizing Jayla's thoughts. "Grant Weston is your father."

That was what it took. Jayla leaned over and threw up the inside of her stomach in some nearby bushes. To think she had had sexual encounters with her father. The thought was beyond sick, and she could do nothing but gag, as if rejecting the feel of his dick in her mouth. "You're lying," she said between snatches of breath. Her eyes overflowed with tears as she turned to face Sheila.

Sheila nodded to confirm the allegation. "She showed me the paternity test earlier," she said. "I didn't know, Jayla. I didn't know when I came to you about him."

"She didn't know," Patricia agreed. "No one knew. Not Grant. Not Jillian. No one."

"Why?" Jayla screamed. "How could you do something like that? You don't know how my mother struggled because we had no one. And what about me, Patricia? How do you think I felt not ever knowing who my father was?"

Patricia sighed. "Yeah, I bet that was rough," she said, her tone condescending. "It was nothing personal, Puma. I didn't even know you. I knew I loved Grant, though, and I couldn't have Jillian taking that away from me. And it worked. Grant saw that Jillian had 'cheated' on him to conceive you, and he left her."

"And it wasn't true?"

Patricia shook her head. "No, she never cheated on Grant, that I know of. But I had managed to make him believe that lie, so it didn't even matter what she said. And I did keep tabs on you. You know, to make sure you were okay."

"And us?" Jayla silently begged her with her eyes to deny the entire thing. "We met in college. You were my professor. You . . . you put me up on the Heartbreaker business. Was that you keeping tabs on me, Patricia?"

Patricia's smile was almost sadistic. "No, that was just me having a little fun. Jillian was dead, but I could definitely get back at her through her precious little girl."

Jayla's eyes watered. How could she have been deceived for so long? How could she have fallen for such a vengeful tactic, one that had ruined her entire life? How could she not have seen through Patricia's chicanery? She really had thought the woman loved her and cared about her. Damn, was Patricia just that good, or had she been just that stupid?

"But I don't understand." Jayla didn't care that she was crying as she pushed to hear the whole truth. "How did you do all of that and Sheila still married Grant? That doesn't make sense."

"Well . . ." Patricia rose now, shoving her hands inside her jacket pockets. "Needless to say, I got in some trouble. I was a little bit of a ho before I met Grant, so some things I did came back to bite me, and I went to jail for a few months. I told Sheila to keep an eye on him for me while I was gone. He had just left Jillian, you see, and I knew it was only a matter of time before he would be proposing to me, now that he needed a wife." She cut her eyes at Sheila. "Some people just don't know how to follow directions."

"It wasn't like that," Sheila said. "Jayla, I told you on the boat that we married out of convenience. We didn't even love each other like that. Patricia was my friend, but she was gone, and Grant told me he could never be with her, because she was bad for his public image. He knew he wanted to be a senator, and maybe the president one day. How could he do that with a ho as his first lady?"

Patricia chuckled. "Touché."

Sheila went on. "I didn't think there was any bad blood between us. So I came to her about my issues with Grant, and she told me she couldn't do it, but she had someone who could."

Jayla nodded as the puzzle pieces begin to click into place. "Me."

"In exchange for her help, she told me she was in some deep trouble and needed help faking her death," Sheila continued. "So I told her I would help her. That was it. All this other shit about her personal revenge with you, Jayla, and you being Grant's daughter . . . Well, I didn't know anything about all that. After I saw the photos had been leaked, and we ruled out Carl as the traitor, I knew Patricia had done it, since she wasn't really dead. So, I met her today to confront her about it."

Jayla was stunned into silence. All this time she had thought she couldn't trust Sheila. The ultimate deceiver, the ultimate *heartbreaker*, had been giggling and grinning in her face the entire time.

Patricia had just wanted to humiliate her because of the resentment she harbored toward her mother. Everything had been for the sake of revenge.

Patricia took a breath. "I'll always love Grant, but now he knows he shouldn't have fucked me over. Twice. He thinks he can get all successful and leave me in the wind. Well, I showed him he couldn't have anything without me. I stripped everything from him and left him with nothing. And since I'm dead, it's not like he'll be able to find me anyway. Now we can part ways and pretend none of the past month ever happened. It's been fun, ladies." She turned on her heel and sauntered down the sidewalk, a noticeable pep in each elongated stride.

Sheila shook her head. "Oh, it's not that easy, Patricia," she murmured, so low that Jayla wasn't even sure she had actually heard the quiet threat.

But Jayla was already silently calculating her own plan of action to get back at that scheming, sneaky bitch once and for all.

CHAPTER TWENTY

Jasmine

The squeak of the hinges echoed off the empty walls as Jasmine shifted and twisted, searching for some modicum of comfort on the flat mattress. It didn't help that her wrist was handcuffed to the iron bed. Defeated, she sat up and rested her bare feet on the cold linoleum. The gray sweat suit did nothing to protect her skin from the chill in the room. With a smack of her lips, Jasmine pulled at the cuffs, then hissed as the metal bit into her flesh.

Bastards called themselves punishing her for her latest outburst. She had hauled off and attacked one of the nurses after the girl had tried to shove some medicine down her throat. But she would rather be in the psych hospital than at the jail any day.

After her arrest, Jasmine had toggled between calling Kendra and calling Grant, but neither had answered. She'd been pissed because that had meant she couldn't get her hands on the bail money she needed. She hadn't been able to bring herself to call her parents. No matter how much she cried innocent, neither Jackie nor Quentin would ever let her hear the end of it. Plus, their broke asses wouldn't have the fifty thousand dollars needed to put up for bail, which was set at half a million dollars. So rather than sit in jail for the three weeks until her arraignment, Jasmine had played up her crazy, which hadn't been too hard, since she hadn't been able to stomach being around those dykes all day. After a few days she'd been transferred to a nearby mental health institution.

So far, between the group therapy and the counseling sessions that they required daily, it hadn't been too bad. The rooms were halfway decent, and everyone pretty much kept to themselves. With the exception of the occasional schizo bashing her head against the windows or stripping in the middle of the recreation room, it was tolerable. But, damn, she was pissed that she hadn't made bail and that no one had answered her calls. By now she should've been at her own home, on her own sheets, trying to round up the best lawyer money or sex could come by so she could get out of this mess.

Murder Marcus? No way in hell. Tracy maybe, but never her Marcus. Either way, the police claimed to have some evidence that she had tampered with his brakes, and they maintained that her fingerprints were all over the car. None of it made sense, but no one was trying to hear that. She just needed to figure out what to do. She hadn't been able to get her hands on the money she had saved thanks to Grant's generosity, so she had been handed some bum-ass public lawyer, who seemed more interested in her titties than in actually helping her win her case. If only Kendra would answer her damn phone. Jasmine didn't know what the fuck her problem was, but she was supposed to be her friend, and the chick hadn't bothered even to visit her to see if she was still alive. She didn't even know what was going on with her daughter, Gabby.

The footsteps coming toward her room had Jasmine stretching her stiffened muscles. She glanced toward the barred window, noted the beautiful purple sky, signaling the transition to night. "Assholes," she murmured angrily through clenched teeth. They had left her in there for hours. She swallowed the stream of curses already itching on her tongue. She had become accustomed to the small conveniences of the behavioral health center, so she knew she needed to be good to get through the rest of her time there. She focused on the approaching steps and waited patiently as the locks were clicked out of place.

A nurse opened the door and stepped to the side to allow Jasmine's psychiatrist through. Jasmine tried not to squeal from excitement. Her visits with Dr. Joseph Hammond were one of the few things keeping her sane in this nuthouse. He was African, so his accent was sexy, but it was so thick that she sometimes had trouble understanding him. It didn't help that she was always distracted by that smooth midnight complexion of his, which contrasted with those gorgeous teeth and made his smile look that much brighter.

"Heard you got into some trouble," Joseph said as the door closed behind him. He held up the key, letting it dangle from his middle finger. "Promise to be good if I let you go?"

Jasmine grinned. "Absolutely," she said.

As soon as he unlocked the cuffs, she threw her arms around his neck and pulled him on top of her on the bed.

"Wait a minute. Wait a minute, my princess." Joseph chuckled as her tongue sought his mouth. "Not here."

"Why not? It's kind of a turn-on, don't you think?" The bed squeaked under their weight as she wrapped her legs around his waist.

Joseph gave in for a moment, briefly wrapping his thick tongue around hers and swallowing her moan. She felt his dick harden between her legs, and she squirmed anxiously. "It's too loud here," he murmured against her mouth. At the same time, his fingers slipped under the elastic waistband of her pants. "But I may be able to appease you for now."

She gasped as his knuckles caressed her moist slit before he dipped his fingers inside. She was already warm and wet, and her lips gripped his fingers as he stroked the ridges of her walls. She squirmed and gyrated her hips against his hand as he began fingering her. Knowing how she liked it, Joseph positioned his fingers to play in her pussy while he inserted his thumb into her booty hole. She bit back a moan and closed her eyes. He quickened his pace.

"Yes," she whispered. "Damn, please. Don't stop."

When he used his other hand to flick the swollen nub of her clit and gently squeeze it between his thumb and index finger, Jasmine screamed. Soon her nectar drenched his hand and wet her sweatpants. He pulled his hand out, and she felt the sting of her waistband as it slapped her abdomen.

"You were too loud." Joseph scowled as he stood up and used his handkerchief to wipe her nut from his fingers. "They're going to come back, and you'll get us both in trouble."

Jasmine chuckled, still high from her postorgasmic euphoria. "Fuck them," she mumbled. "They all can kiss my ass."

He tossed the damp handkerchief on her chest. "Clean yourself up," he said. "I'll see if they can let you out of here in another hour or so."

Jasmine watched him make his way to the door before she suddenly remembered why she needed him. "Joseph. I need your help," she said. "I need you to make a phone call for me. I need to reach someone."

"Why don't you just call them?"

"Because she won't come if I call," Jasmine answered. "But maybe if you call for me and explain how serious it is for her to come, maybe she will."

Joseph frowned. "What do you mean, serious?"

"Well . . ." Jasmine grinned slyly. "I was wondering if you could call and make it sound like it's really bad in here for me. Like I'm on suicide watch or something. You're a doctor. Give her a list of mental issues that may give her a reason to be concerned. I just need her to come."

"Um, all right." Joseph's agreement was a reluctant one, but it was an agreement, nonetheless.

Jasmine smiled inwardly. Kendra and Grant were ignoring her, but there was one more person she could call. She just hoped Jayla was still as naive as she used to be, because Jasmine needed her if she wanted to get out of this place.

One hour turned into overnight. By the time they finally let Jasmine out, she was cramped from sleeping in such an awkward position. Not to mention hungry, and she felt like she needed a week's worth of baths.

"You have a visitor," the nurse said, taking her by the arm.

Jasmine grinned. She was glad Jayla had come. Now, if she played her cards right, she would be out of there in a matter of hours.

She showered and changed into a fresh sweat suit, and after a quick breakfast of pancakes and fruit, she was escorted to the sunroom. Wicker furniture with plush cushions adorned the room, and with all the potted plants, the air in the room smelled like that of a garden. Floor-to-ceiling windows exposed the overcast sky outside, and as Jasmine took a seat on the sofa's aged cushions, a few droplets of rain splattered on the glass and harmonized with the soft jazz pouring through the speakers in the ceiling.

The door opened, and Jasmine turned in her seat. After she caught sight of the visitor, her eyes darkened from anger. Not Jayla. It was Kendra. An empty-handed Kendra at that.

Jasmine jumped to her feet. "Damn. Look who finally decided to show up," she snapped.

"You've got some nerve coming at me like I owe you a visit," Kendra lashed back, slapping her hand on her hip. "You're in here over some stupid crap you pulled. I didn't even have to come today."

"Oh, excuse me. I thought you were my best friend."

Kendra rolled her eyes and took a seat in the chair opposite the sofa Jasmine had occupied. "You know, I'm sick of you always playing the damn selfish victim, Jasmine," she said, her voice calmer now, despite the agitation creasing her face. "Everything I've done for you . . . I can't believe you would even sit up here and say something like that to me. Like I haven't been here for you this entire time."

"Where have you been lately, Kendra?" Jasmine threw up her hands and gestured wildly to the room. "Where have you been when I needed you most? I've been in this place for damn near two weeks. How am I supposed to feel?"

Kendra lowered her eyes, and when she lifted them again, they were filled with suspicion. She hadn't wanted to bring up the situation, but not knowing was stressing her out. "I couldn't bring myself to come, Jasmine," she admitted. "Hell, you were arrested and dragged out of that house for murder. I didn't know what to think."

"I can't believe you believe that, Kendra," Jasmine replied, her voice high from outrage. She collapsed on the sofa. "You know I didn't kill nobody. Especially Marcus. I loved him."

Kendra shook her head either from the shock of it all or Jasmine's denial. "I just don't believe you got yourself in this mess," she said. "And when you left, I see Senator Grant Weston in your bedroom. All this time, he was your sugar daddy? I'm just . . . disgusted by you, Jasmine. I don't know what to think of you anymore."

"Kendra, it's not as bad as you think," Jasmine pleaded. "Don't think of me as some monster. I did what I had to do to get by. I don't know where shit went sour."

"Probably when you were dating Marcus. Then you met his dad, and he became your sugar daddy, and then you killed Marcus to get him out of your way."

"Ugh. Is that what the media is saying?" Jasmine shook her head in disbelief.

"Oh, they're spinning several stories with you as the headline," Kendra revealed. "Another one is you found out about Marcus's wife, Tracy, and meant to kill her, but he just so happened to be there. But I can tell you this. Nowhere is anyone saying that you two were together. They say it was all in your head and you are just crazy." Kendra's eyes panned the room. "Exhibit A."

Jasmine rose to her feet and began to pace the room. Shit had gotten out of control. The judicial system killed murderers. She couldn't die over something she didn't do. She just couldn't. She ignored the rising fear and racked her brain for a solution. "That's why you have to help me,

Kendra," she said, turning to face her friend. "This is ugly, but I can't do anything from in here. I need to get out, so I can handle this."

Kendra's face twisted into a confused frown. "I don't know, Jasmine. I think this is the best place for you. You know, I've been wanting you to get some help for the longest. Do you have different therapy sessions and stuff?"

"Kendra, fuck that," Jasmine snapped, rolling her eyes. "I need to get out of here. Do you hear me? I'm in some real trouble. Look, my bail is set at five hundred thousand dollars. There is some money stashed away in the house. My spare key is buried in a box to the left of the front porch. Right in front of the plant. There is a bag of money in the Hungry-Man TV dinner box in the freezer. Not sure how much is in there, but it should be close to fifty thousand dollars. If you need more, you should be able to get the rest from Grant."

"Get more from Grant? I was afraid they don't let you watch the news in here." At Jasmine's frown, Kendra reached in her purse and pulled out a folded-up newspaper.

Jasmine read the headline, and she felt like the world had fallen off its axis. Her vision blurred from dizziness as the words jumped out to punch her in the gut. *Transvestite. His daughter. Sex.* She took a deep breath, and then her eyes scanned the article. Her blood ran cold when she saw the name. *Jayla. Grant's daughter*. The paper slipped from her fingers. "Jayla is Grant's daughter?" she asked, the words trembling on her lips.

"Yeah."

Jasmine shook her head. She couldn't bring herself to believe it. She had slept with her *grand-father*? Her heart wouldn't let her believe it. Even as her mind raced to make sense of the news, she just refused to believe it. She didn't even realize Kendra had stood to leave until the woman was already at the door.

Kendra turned to eye her friend, feeling almost sympathetic about her situation. Almost. Part of her had already given up on Jasmine. Especially after their last argument. Kendra had tried to reason with her, but Jasmine had been dead set on doing whatever the hell she wanted to, and because of that, she had gotten herself in this mess. So maybe this was Jasmine's wake-up call. She had had it easy for too long, thanks to people like Grant laying out the red carpet for her. Perhaps now she needed to feel the weight of the world, like the rest of them.

"You know . . . ," Kendra said, and she had Jasmine looking at her, still in somewhat of a daze. "I've been here almost an hour, and you have yet to ask about Gabrielle."

Jasmine was still overcome by the reality of the shit about Grant, so she couldn't even muster interest in the subject of Gabrielle. "How is she?" she asked absently.

Kendra's smile was one of pity. "I'm going to do what I need to do," she said. "You can't be the mother that baby needs. And I don't want the responsibility of raising a child. So, consider this your goodbye, because you'll never see her again."

"Are you going to bring my bail money?" Jasmine said. She couldn't be concerned about the baby. She had bigger issues to confront.

"Nope," Kendra admitted, with a smirk. "I'll handle that money for you as well. Since I'm so jealous of you and I'm hating, and you so freely threw in my face how you didn't have to work for shit and I did, I'll take care of that money. Don't worry. I'll spend it good for you."

"You fucking bitch!" Jasmine vaulted over the sofa and would've dragged Kendra down to the floor by her neck if she hadn't already disappeared through the door leading back into the building.

Jasmine snatched the door open, and two male nurses immediately grabbed her arms and hauled her backward. "Let me go!" she screamed as they hoisted her in the air. "Let me go! That bitch is going to steal my money. Please!"

She grunted as they slammed her on her back on the floor and struggled to take hold of her flailing arms and legs. From her vantage point on the sunroom floor, Jasmine caught sight of Kendra disappearing down the hall. But then she felt the prick of a needle in her arm, and everything faded to black.

CHAPTER TWENTY-ONE

Jayla

Diary Entry 34:

I don't play fair. Revenge is not meant to be. Strategy Part 1: Divide. Bitch has underestimated me. Destroy or be destroyed. There is only room for one. Strategy Part 2: Conquer. I'll be the last one standing when all is said and done.

Shit is dirty; feelings are hurt. But I don't give a damn about the pain. As long as the shit works.

All is fair in sex and revenge.

Signed,
Patricia

Jayla closed the cover of the diary and could only shake her head. Her mind was all the way blown at Patricia's confession. The bitch had been the ultimate deceiver. And to think she had been tangled in Patricia's web of deception since before she was born. She had always been cautious. Hell, Patricia had taught her to be that way. But meanwhile, she was the one hiding in the shadows, feeding Jayla faux love, affection, and wise words as a means of distraction.

Angry tears fell from Jayla's eyes to dampen the papers strewn in front of her on the kitchen table. She had found them among Patricia's things in the house and had decided to take a closer look. As if maybe there was something there that contradicted the harsh reality of Patricia's treacherousness. That maybe, just maybe, she'd discover that Patricia's words had been a lie, and that she couldn't possibly have been so deceptive and cruel for so long. But the content of Patricia's drawers had served only as a confirmation instead of a rebuttal. She had leafed through pictures, phone records, dinner receipts. Records of flights and hotel stays, ultrasound pictures, and gas receipts. And it had pained her to see pictures of Jillian. Some were of her alone; some, of her in the arms of Grant.

Patricia had followed them and documented their every move. The woman was psychotic. Jayla hadn't found any pictures to substantiate Patricia's claim that she and Grant had had some kind of romantic relationship. And the more she'd read, the more she'd realized that Jillian had been his true love and Patricia had been the side bitch. It certainly coincided with Patricia's feelings about men and trust. Patricia had been a Heartbreaker before she had even realized what the hell she was doing. She'd just set out to ruin lives. And she had definitely succeeded.

The phone rang, pulling Jayla away from her dreadful thoughts. She glanced at the clock before answering the call and putting the phone to her ear. "Hello?" she said after clearing the tears in her throat.

"Jayla?"

She frowned at the African accent. Probably another reporter. The leeches still were trying to drag her through the mud over the allegations. "Who is this?"

"This is Dr. Joseph Hammond," he said. "I am a therapist here at the Angel Wings Behavioral Health Center. I'm calling on behalf of Jasmine Morgan."

Jayla held her breath, waiting for him to continue. *This should be good.*

"Jasmine is in some trouble down here, and I was wondering if you could come over for a visit. She has been asking about you."

"Me?" Jayla laughed. "Get real. That bitch doesn't even like me."

"Well, she is in desperate need of some attention. She has made several unsuccessful attempts to commit suicide."

"It would serve her right," Jayla snapped.

"Please, Ms. Morgan," Dr. Hammond said, pressing. "She requested you specifically. She's on suicide watch, and I'm afraid she may try again. She started rambling on about making amends and righting her wrongs. I think you should at least hear her out."

Just then Jayla heard the dull roar of a car engine, and she glanced out the kitchen bay window. "I'll think about," she said absently. "I have to go." She hung up and stood up just as Patricia came sailing through the back door, bringing in a burst of cold air with her.

"I'm so surprised you called, Puma," she said with a smirk as she pulled off her gloves.

"I'm even more surprised you came," Jayla said, struggling to keep the disgust out of her voice.

"Well, you said it was urgent, and I figured what the hell." Habit had Patricia strolling to the refrigerator. She opened the refrigerator and pulled out the sangria she always kept chilling on the door. "Besides," she said, turning, with a devilish glint in her eye, "I think we kind of ended things on a sour note. Before I leave town, I said I could see my Puma one last time."

"It's the least you can do," Jayla mumbled, easing back into the chair. "You owe me, Patricia. You took my fucking life from me. Don't you care?"

"All is fair in sex and revenge," she said with a shrug.

The hurt stabbed Jayla with a vengeance, as the woman had quoted a line from the last diary entry of hers that Jayla had read. Patricia had absolutely no remorse, and Jayla knew that was what hurt worse than the rest of it.

"My mother wasn't the other woman, was she?" Jayla asked, swiping the pictures of Grant and Jillian together in Patricia's direction. They flew off the kitchen table and littered the floor at her feet, and Patricia didn't so much as spare a glance at the mess.

"Whether she was or I was, what difference does it make? I loved him."

"But you took him from my mother. She had him first."

"Oh, she had him first," Patricia mocked in a baby voice before taking a swig of her drink. "You sound like a little brat crying over her toys in the sandbox. Grow the fuck up. Haven't I taught you better than that?"

Jayla buried her face in her hands and let the tears spill. Her heart had damn near burst from her chest, it was beating so hard. "You ain't taught me shit but betrayal, deceit, and how to lie my ass off, Patricia."

"And look where it got you, sweetie." Patricia gestured wildly toward the house. "You should be proud of your accomplishments. Look at how much money you were making before you fucked up and went to jail. Look at how much Sheila probably paid you. You're set."

Jayla shook her head. Patricia's mindset was absolutely insane beyond belief. But then again, the years had twisted her into some deranged monster, whom she had hidden under money and a beautiful face. Even worse, Jayla couldn't even bring herself to look at the woman she had once looked up to as her mentor and mother figure. She had killed her own mother, thinking Jillian was being deceptive, and had run right into the arms of the devil herself. And Patricia had managed to devour her vulnerable ass whole.

A crashing sound had both women's heads snapping to the door. About five or six masked intruders dressed in all black burst into the kitchen, their guns drawn.

Jayla lifted her hands in the air as her eyes grew large. *What the hell?* She looked over at Patricia, who had her arms up, a similar look of panic etched on her pale face.

"Ladies, calm down," a familiar voice said, and the group seemed to part like the Red Sea. Dreena stepped forward, two guns of her own in the waist of her jeans and a red scarf tied around her braids.

She had a blunt between her fingers as she looked at Jayla.

"Well, well, well." Dreena smiled as she stepped into Jayla's face. The smell of weed seemed to come from her pores. "Long time no see, Jayla."

Jayla kept her lips pursed as she glanced at the guns still pointed between her and Patricia. She doubted Dreena actually expected her to respond.

"We're going to make this quick," Dreena said, still holding Jayla's gaze with a menacing scowl. "Let's off this bitch, take everything of value, and get the fuck out of here."

The guns clicked, and suddenly, all of them were aimed at Patricia. She paled, and her head whipped in Jayla's direction. The question was clear in her eyes, but she dared not open her mouth to verbalize it.

Dreena smirked and planted a friendly kiss on Jayla's lips. "Bitch, put your damn hands down. You called us, remember?"

Jayla let out the breath she had been holding. She relaxed into a smile and rose to her feet. "Yeah, but you and your bitches come busting in here like y'all about to shoot first and ask questions later. Busting my windows and shit."

Dreena laughed. "Oh, that was for effect."

Jayla shifted her eyes to Patricia's and smiled. "Oh, you don't recognize Big D, or Dreena, here, do you?"

Still confused, Patricia slid her gaze to Dreena.

"That's because the bitch was too busy taking my money and not repaying it to know what the fuck I look like," Dreena snapped. "Oh, but we got body bags for bitches like you." She turned back to Jayla and reached for her hand. "But seriously, though, my fault for having my girls fuck you up before. But when you called and told me this was the bitch that got you out of jail, trying to pin shit on me, you know I had to roll through."

Jayla nodded. Dreena's name had been scribbled on all of Patricia's debt receipts and gambling stuff in her drawers. Apparently, her head was worth a lot more than Jayla's. So, Jayla hadn't hesitated to call up Dreena and make an exchange. "So, we good?" she asked.

Dreena slapped her hand and pulled her in for an embrace. "Yeah, we good," she agreed. "But I still get anything I want up in this muthafucka too, right? Seeing as you did leave my ass in jail and shit."

"Yeah, go on," Jayla said with a light laugh. She nodded toward Patricia. "Just make sure her ass is gone for good."

"Oh, no doubt. You told me her ass is supposed to be dead already, anyway." Dreena nodded, and two of her girls ran off to begin racking up on stuff in the house.

Jayla couldn't even bring herself to look at Patricia. She just wanted the bitch out of her sight.

"Puma." Patricia was in tears now, as the reality of the situation had begun to settle in. "You're going to just let these loan sharks kill me?"

"Damn right," Jayla said without hesitation. "When they're through with you, you're going to wish you did die of cancer, bitch. I'm gonna let them do this for my mother, for Grant, for me. For every life you fucked up just by being here."

"Oh yeah, I'm going to have fun torturing this bitch." Dreena clapped her hands together, as if she were giddy with excitement.

Someone knocked Patricia in the head with a gun, and she grunted and collapsed to the floor. Blood spilled from her head.

"Hey, hey," Dreena yelled. "Bitch, wait until we get where we going. Jaye said she didn't want no damn blood in the fucking house. Shit!" Obediently, two of Dreena's girls dragged a limp Patricia out of the house by her arms. Dreena shook her head. "Damn newbies," she mumbled.

Jayla nodded and glanced at the blood that spotted the kitchen floor. For some reason, the sight brought her an overpowering sense of relief.

CHAPTER TWENTY-TWO

Jasmine

Because she had tripped out, Jasmine had to spend three more days being closely monitored. She wasn't allowed to join the other patients, and she had to go to twice as many therapy sessions, plus an anger management class once a week. The shit was nerve-racking wasting away in there while she had no contact with the outside world. Her mind had rejected the whole Grant fiasco, but it wasn't like she could keep up with what was going on. The patients weren't allowed to watch the news. Instead, the staff kept movies and music on repeat. Like they were in a bubble. Jasmine could easily see how even if people weren't crazy going in, they damn sure went crazy while they were in there.

So, she was surprised when a nurse pulled her from recreational therapy one afternoon to say she had another visitor. Jasmine was confused when the nurse walked her to a wheelchair and nudged her into the seat. Then she handcuffed her to the chair.

Jasmine rolled her eyes. “Really?” she snapped as the nurse began wheeling her to the sunroom.

“Just a precaution, Ms. Morgan,” she said with a bright smile. “After your last visit, you’re lucky we allow you to have any visitors at all.”

They approached the sunroom, and Jasmine was surprised to see Jayla standing next to the window, her arms crossed over her chest as she leaned against the glass. For the first time, Jasmine saw an image of herself in the older woman, and the thought brought back a host of memories that she couldn’t help but despise her for. And to add insult to injury, Jayla would come up in there looking glamorous in her skinny-leg jeans and Donna Karan sweater. Jasmine turned up her lips in hatred. Jayla just had to outshine her. That was probably the only reason the bitch had agreed to come.

The nurse maneuvered her wheelchair into the sunroom and angled it next to the sofa before leaving them alone. For a while, they maintained the distance between them and stared menacingly at each other. Then, to Jasmine’s surprise, Jayla’s face broke into a smile.

“Look at you,” she said. “I wondered what I would do when I saw you again.”

Jasmine chuckled. “Is that so? You think you gone beat my ass while I’m tied to a fucking wheelchair, Jayla? That’s low. Even for you.”

"What do you want, little girl?" Jayla's voice was pleasant enough, but it was clear that anger simmered below the surface. "You've got some nerve having me come down here like we're best friends."

Jasmine sighed. She would need to bite back her harsh comebacks if she wanted to pull this off. She didn't give a damn about Jayla any more than Jayla cared about her, but she couldn't very well verbalize that if she was going to get Jayla to fork over the bail money. "I think it's finally time for us to talk," she said, her tone calm and as convincing as she make it. "Yes, I asked you down here for a reason, and I appreciate you coming. So, can we talk? For real?"

Jayla's eyebrow lifted from doubt, but she didn't speak as she slid into a nearby chair. She crossed her legs and arms, and her entire demeanor exuded the defensiveness she probably felt. "Fine," she said. "Talk."

"Well, first off, let me please apologize, Jayla," Jasmine began. She fixed her face and tried to force tears as she spat out the first bullshit that came to mind. "I was wrong on so many levels. I can't even begin to think about how much I hurt you with everything I did. I guess part of me was angry. The abortion . . . then to find out you were my biological mother. Then . . . I found out about my HIV . . ."

The tears fell now, big and sloppy, and she could see Jayla's face had fallen. She plowed on through with shaky breaths. "I'm so sorry. There is no excuse for my behavior. None. But I've been to counseling in here, and I've done some soul-searching. And I've learned I can't change the past, so I shouldn't dwell on it. So now I'm trying to do what I need to do to move on from all my mistakes to a better future. And I . . ." She paused, sniffing for effect. "And I want you in my future, Jayla. As my friend. And as my mother."

The weight of her words could be felt in the room, and Jasmine could've sworn she saw Jayla blink back her own set of tears. She chuckled to herself inwardly. Damn, she needed a fucking Oscar for that one.

Jayla looked away and sighed. "Jasmine, I . . . I don't know what to say," she said. "For a long time, I wasn't sure if I could trust you. But then I realized you were the spitting image of me, and I had no one to blame for your issues but myself. I refused to take that responsibility. And for that, I'm sorry."

"I've always looked up to you, Jayla. Always. I've always admired the person you were. Maybe that was part of the reason I strived so much to be like you. It's no excuse. But now I'm willing to do whatever it takes for us to grow together. No more secrets. No more lies. Just an open, honest, and trusting relationship." She was laying it on heavy, but Jayla was sopping the shit up like gravy. Whatever it took.

"I would love that," Jayla said with a smile, and then she walked over and embraced her daughter.

Jasmine hugged her back with her one free arm, and for a moment, the embrace felt genuine. Completely genuine.

"So, what is going on?" Jayla sat down on the sofa, beside the wheelchair, and took Jasmine's hand in her own. "What's all this I hear about you being arrested for murder?"

Jasmine sighed and looked away. "I don't know what the hell is going on. They claim they have some evidence of me tampering with my boyfriend's car, but it is not true."

"We saw each other at the funeral," Jayla said, more to herself. "Was that your boyfriend? Marcus?"

Jasmine nodded and sighed with regret. "I loved him," she admitted. "I really loved that boy. And he loved me. We were going to be together. There's no way I would've ever killed Marcus."

"I hate to break this to you," Jayla said. "But Marcus was after me. I think he was using you to get to me."

Jasmine's eyebrows crinkled together. "What?" she asked, genuinely confused.

"Right before you . . . right before I got locked up, Marcus and his sister-in-law, Lauren, held me hostage in my apartment," Jayla explained, shuddering as she relived the moment. "Lauren was Tracy's sister, and apparently, they had some nasty-ass love triangle going on. I don't know, but either way, Lauren and Marcus were going to kill me. Me and Lauren got into a fight over the gun, and I shot her. She died. But Marcus got away."

Jasmine's face reflected the shock she felt upon hearing this story, but she was already blocking out the words. Just like this bitch to tell her some bullshit, she thought. No, her Marcus loved her. Of course, Jayla's selfish ass would try to steal that little piece of her happiness. But instead of voicing that, Jasmine gasped, playing into Jayla's little delusion. "Are you serious?"

Jayla nodded, lowering her eyes. "They killed your aunt Jocelyn," she murmured.

Jasmine eyed the woman in disgust. How she could sit up here and tell those kind of lies? She was absolutely sick. She should be the one strapped to a wheelchair. Yet here Jasmine was while sick bitches like Jayla freely roamed the earth. It wasn't fair. She bit back her harsh reply and instead shook her head, her face fixed to reflect the shock she knew Jayla was searching for. "Damn. I don't know what to say," she said. "That is crazy. I am so sorry."

Jayla gave her hand a reassuring squeeze. "It's okay. I'm dealing with it."

"I'm trying to deal too," Jasmine said, as if she were speaking to herself. "But it's so hard. I need to get out of here."

"Well, what's the next step? Are you waiting on a court date or something?"

"Sort of. I have bail set, and my friend was supposed to bring the money, but . . ." Jasmine rolled her eyes. "Go figure. The chick ran off with all my money while leaving me in here to rot."

"Damn. Well, how much is your bail?"

Jasmine widened her eyes, ready to milk this thing like Bessie. "Oh, no, Jayla. I couldn't ask you to do that for me. It's way too much money."

Jayla waved her hand. "How much?" she repeated.

"Fifty thousand dollars."

"No problem." Jayla didn't even bat an eye. She stood and pulled her cell phone from her pocket. "'I'll post it for you."

Jasmine waited as Jayla began swiping her swift fingers on the phone's touch screen. "Are you sure?" she asked meekly.

"Jasmine, you're my daughter," Jayla said, not even bothering to look up from her phone. "What kind of slum mother would I be to leave you in here? We need to get you out and work on building a case so we can get you off. Do you have a lawyer?"

"Not really."

"I'll handle that for you. Let me go talk to the folks here." She stooped down, and to Jasmine's surprise, she kissed her forehead. "I love you, Jasmine," she said, so low that Jasmine almost felt the love oozing from the words. "I've always loved you. Just know that . . . I never wanted to give you up for adoption."

Jayla left her alone, and Jasmine rolled her eyes. She could almost feel the slight tug on her heart from the woman's words. And maybe in another life, they could've had the whole Tina Knowles and Beyoncé thing. But that shit was long gone now. She couldn't wait for Jayla to get her out of here, so she could get her life together. But she would need to play the beloved daughter for a while longer. Getting out of here was the first step. Then she needed to suck her mother for as much money as she could, since she would need it when she went on the run. Jasmine had decided that she couldn't take a chance on the judicial system. She would be better off on her own. And with her African prince, Dr. Joseph Hammond, she just might be able to establish a new life as one of his new concubines in the motherland.

"So, I heard you are getting discharged later," Joseph said, holding Jasmine from behind as she sat naked on his lap. His dark skin was an erotic contrast to her lighter complexion as his fingers played with her erect nipples.

Jasmine turned and wrapped her arms around his neck. "Are you going to miss me?" she said with a pout.

"You know I am, my princess." Joseph lifted his limp dick and rested it on her thigh. "And he will too."

Jasmine laughed. She had already thoroughly satisfied the good doctor. She hated sucking all that damn skin on his uncircumcised dick, and she had to admit, it felt a little . . . stuffed every time he pounded her pussy. But it was dick just the same, and he definitely knew how to work his Mandingo. And if avoiding this murder rap meant she allowed him to bust her wide open in every therapy session, well, dammit, she was going to follow the doctor's orders. She wasn't going to jail. Plus, Joseph would always boast about how comfortable his wives were. He had mentioned he had plenty of land in Africa and had built each one of them a little mini mansion on the property. He always sent money home to take care of them, so none of them had to do anything but raise his kids, spend his money, and sex him every time he flew over for a visit. It sounded like a winning lottery ticket to her.

"I was thinking about something, baby," she whispered, her breath tickling his skin, as she nuzzled in the crook of his neck. "We talked about you taking me back to Africa when I got out of here. Meeting your family. Getting in touch with my heritage."

"We did. But I didn't think that was a consideration for you, my princess."

"It is." Jasmine angled her face to look him dead in his eyes. "I think I'm falling in love with you, Joseph Hammond. I don't think I've ever felt like this about anyone."

She had obviously said the right things, because Joseph smiled, his eyes squinting with the rise of his cheeks. "That's good to know," he said. "I wouldn't mind bringing you back and marrying you. You're young, and you're thick. You have a perfect body for making me some babies."

He slapped her thigh, and Jasmine winced at the sting. She kept a smile planted on her face. "How soon can we go?"

" Do you have a passport?"

"No."

"We have to get you one. That can take a few months. I leave for Africa again in three months, but your stuff should be processed in time."

Jasmine shook her head vehemently. Three months was three months too long. "Can't we go sooner?" she asked, pressing him. "Like tomorrow?"

Joseph kissed her shoulder and rested his cheek on her back. "Let's work on getting your passport expedited, and maybe I can send you and fly out to meet you when I wrap up some business. Let's talk about this over dinner. Why don't you go home and pack and come stay with me tonight? We can work out the details."

Though she was not completely satisfied, Jasmine nodded. It wasn't enough, but at least it was something. "Okay. Give me a kiss goodbye for now."

Taking the hint, Joseph opened her legs, wrapped them around his neck, and gave Jasmine's pussy a passionate kiss. He flicked his tongue over the lips, which were still wet with their mix of cum from moments before. "Until tonight," he said.

Jasmine stood and quickly got dressed. Her thighs were sticky with her juices, but she didn't bother to shower. She wanted no more of that generic bar soap that smelled like a hospital and never made suds no matter how much she scrubbed. No, in just a few short hours, she would be home, in her own Jacuzzi tub, with her candles and peppermint-scented bath salts. That thought alone had her nearly prancing as she made the trek back to the residential wing.

She hadn't actually expected Jayla to buy into her bullshit. But apparently, she had really sold it, because no sooner had Jayla left the visitation than Jasmine got word that her bail had been posted and she would be discharged from the behavioral health center. That left her with a little over a week until her arraignment hearing. And a little over a week to get the fuck out of the United States.

Jasmine joined the other patients in the lounge and settled into one of the reclining chairs to wait. This area was used for what they called "recreational therapy." It was set up like a living room, complete with numerous sofas and chairs and throw pillows that clashed horribly with the dated floral upholstery. A boarded-up fireplace served more as a decoration, but it added minor charm to the quaint space. The only modern convenience was the flat-screen TV mounted to the wall above the mantel. Now, scenes from an old movie danced on the screen, but no one paid attention. Though the television was meant to encourage for interaction, everyone kept to themselves in here, and that was why Jasmine loved it.

"Jasmine Morgan?" The nurse's authoritative tone had Jasmine freezing. Damn, was she in trouble? "You're ready," she said with a bright smile.

Jasmine sighed in relief and rose from the recliner to follow the nurse down the hall. They reached the discharge desk, and Jasmine waited impatiently for two staff members to complete the necessary paperwork for her discharge. She was excited, but part of her was trying to ignore the bit of anxiety she was feeling. She didn't know why she felt like something wasn't quite right. After fifteen minutes, Jasmine's paperwork was in order, and she signed all the documents for her release. She was free to go.

Jayla stood in the lobby, and her face brightened as soon as Jasmine entered the room.

Jasmine smiled. "Thank you so much," she said. "You don't know how much this means to me."

"Please don't worry about it." Jayla looped her arm through Jasmine's and steered her toward the exit. "I'm just glad we were able to get you out of there. How do you feel?"

They pushed through the doors, and Jasmine inhaled the freedom. She sighed, basking in the feel of the sun warming her skin. The air even smelled different outside those stale walls. "Much better now," she admitted. "I just want to go home, bathe, and eat some greasy pizza. The food in there felt like I was eating cardboard."

They shared a laugh as they crossed the parking lot. For a moment, for a brief exhilarating moment, it felt sincere and loving. And, Jasmine had to admit, nice. Maybe if this were a different time or a different place and they didn't have so much accumulated shit pitting them against each other, maybe they could be friends again. Jasmine briefly entertained memories of her and Jayla before they were Heartbreakers, before they were mother and daughter, before they were enemies. There was a time when they were actually friends. Jasmine's sigh was wistful as she settled into the front passenger seat of Jayla's BMW. Part of her ached to return to that chapter of her life. When things weren't so complicated. The other part felt the familiar resentment she harbored toward Jayla for pushing her into this . . . twilight zone. It had been nothing but hell ever since.

Now that they were safely ensconced in the BMW, Jasmine decided to ask the question that had been on her mind ever since Kendra revealed the truth. "I saw the newspaper," she said, breaking the silence. Out of the corner of her eye, she caught Jayla's lips tightening.

"I figured you did," Jayla replied, her voice low. "Nothing but a bunch of lies."

"Which part? The part about you sleeping with Grant Weston? Or the part about you being his daughter?"

Jayla thought about the questions. "Both," she said finally. "I had an *arrangement* with Grant. Everything just blew up after Quentin's gay ass got involved."

"Quentin?" Jasmine frowned at the offhand comment. "My dad?" When Jayla didn't respond immediately, Jasmine replayed the words in her head. "He's gay?"

Jayla gave an absent shrug. "Something like that. I figured your mom would've told you."

Jasmine shook her head, refusing to believe it, even though she knew in her heart it was true. To be honest, she had always felt her dad was . . . off. She never would've pinned him for a fruitcake, but now the idea didn't seem too far-fetched. Damn. A laugh rippled through her chest, and she shook her head. The situation was so absurd, it was actually funny.

"Now it's my turn to ask you something," Jayla said, breaking Jasmine's train of thought. "We never discussed the whole thing about . . . us. How do you feel knowing I'm your mother?"

It was Jasmine's turn to shrug as she turned to look out the window. She really didn't want to discuss it. The thought still pissed her off, and she hadn't believed it until Jackie had finally admitted it herself. Jasmine knew all about deception at its finest, but for some reason, knowing that her aunt had raised her and that the woman she thought was her aunt was really her biological mother honestly pained her to her soul.

"I really don't know what to feel, Jayla," she answered, taking care to choose her words wisely. "It's just so weird to think about it." She thought for a minute, then added, "I know I haven't been much of a daughter to you. I guess I'm still just trying to wrap my head around it."

Jayla nodded in understanding. “It’s going to take some getting used to for both of us. But I don’t want you to think of this relationship as any different than how it used to be. You have a mother who loves you.”

Jasmine reached over and took Jayla’s hand in hers. She gave it a comforting squeeze. “Now I have two,” she said with a smile. While Jayla blinked back tears, Jasmine could only shake her head. *Dumb bitch.*

It was evening by the time Jayla had navigated the BMW to Jasmine’s condo. She was seriously on her Mommy Dearest shit, and Jasmine was exhausted from faking that she cared. It was a quarter to seven, and she still needed to bathe and pack so she could get over to Joseph’s house. She had a new life to plan, and she couldn’t wait to leave all this drama behind.

“You sure you don’t need me to stay or anything?” Jayla asked as she pulled into the driveway.

Jasmine laughed to herself. She was doing the most. “I’ll be okay,” she said. “I just need some rest. Thanks again for getting me out of there and bringing me home.”

“Anytime. Why don’t you call me in the morning? Maybe we can do some brunch or something.”

“Sounds great,” Jasmine lied without hesitation and then climbed from the car. She leaned over and added, “I love you.”

"I love you too."

Jasmine closed the door and then waved as Jayla pulled out of the driveway and disappeared down the street. "Damn. Finally," she grumbled to herself as she headed up the walkway.

She hadn't left a porch light on, and she was surprised to find her front door unlocked. "Damn! The least that bitch could do was lock my house up, since she came and stole from me," she murmured. Jasmine stepped inside and pushed the door closed behind her. Now enveloped in complete darkness, she stuck her hand out to search the wall for the light switch. Her hand swiped a picture and sent it flying to the floor, where the glass shattered. Too sleepy to care about either the picture or the light switch, Jasmine walked forward, wincing as broken glass crackled under her sneakers.

She squinted in the dark and struggled to make out the bulky furniture scattered around the living room. Surprise had her mouth dropping open when she saw none. Where was her furniture? Her eyes now accustomed to the dark, she paused at the doorway to the dining room, saw that it, too, was empty, and groaned out loud. Kendra had admitted that she was going to take Jasmine's money, but the bitch had taken her furniture too? Pa-fucking-thetic.

"I figured you would come back."

The voice had Jasmine's sucking in a fearful breath as she whirled around. Thanks to the moonlight that spilled through the window above the sink, she saw that he was standing in the middle of the kitchen, dressed in a black sweat suit. He looked rough, and the light of the moon cast an eerie glow across his face.

Jasmine let out a staggered breath as her heart rate tried to level out. "Grant," she said, relieved. "Baby, I didn't know that was you. What are you doing here? And why are you in the dark?"

"I'm sorry to scare you," he said, moving toward her. "I just . . . damn, baby girl. Everything is messed up right now. I had nowhere else to go. Why were you arrested?" He stood hunched in front of her now, looking so defeated.

"Babe, all that shit was a lie. Someone is trying to pin this on me, but don't worry. We'll get through this."

Grant dissolved in her arms, the weight of his body heavy on her shoulder. Jasmine rubbed his back. She thought Grant had abandoned her too, had believed all that mess like everyone else. Since he was on her side, maybe she could use that to her advantage. He still had connections. If he believed her, he could pull some strings to get her charges dropped. She was still disgusted, now that she knew he was her grandfather, but maybe they could go back to the way they used to be, minus the sex. Though certainly not for as long as she had done it before. But a few months could have her sitting pretty again. Maybe all wasn't lost. Jasmine had learned the art of "faking it" a long time ago.

"I love you," she soothed in his ear. "I love you so much, Big Daddy. Baby girl is right here for you."

"I know." Grant sighed.

Jasmine felt his arms tighten around her body, and she gasped, bracing her hand on his shoulder. "Baby," she whispered, giving him a slight nudge, "baby, you're hurting me." She felt him squeeze harder, those toned arms of his damn near biting into her flesh, as she struggled to pull air into her contracting lungs.

"I loved you," he whispered. "I really thought we could be something. Never in a million years did I think you would take everything from me." His hands eased upward to encircle her neck.

Jasmine shook her head, fighting the wave of dizziness that hit her as his fingers burned into her throat.

"You killed my son," he went on, his tone dark and sinister. "You released those pictures and killed my career. You took every fucking thing from me, you little bitch. You sucked me dry until I had nothing left. There was another woman who hurt me like this a long time ago. I swore to myself it would never happen again. I thought what Jillian did was bad. But you, little girl, hurt me much, much worse."

Tears spewed from her eyes as she struggled to suck in snatches of air, but Grant held on tight. Her mind screamed that it wasn't true, and she moved her lips to voice this. But all that came out was unintelligible gurgling sounds as her spit clogged her throat. She held on to a sliver of hope when she heard the faint sounds of police sirens blaring in the distance. Her eyes bulged as life left her body. Then everything faded to black.

CHAPTER TWENTY-THREE

Jayla

She probably shouldn't have come.

Jayla climbed the stairs to the porch, her hands shoved in the pockets of her coat. She racked her brain for the appropriate words, but her mind drew a foggy blank. She had changed so much that she barely recognized the woman she had grown into. And that meant starting over and coming to terms with what had happened to her all those years ago. That was probably the hardest pill to swallow. A collection of emotions marinated in the pit of her stomach. Anger and hurt were prominent, but she also recognized a trace of grief weighing heavily on her heart. But better to get this over with now.

Jayla pressed the doorbell and listened to the chime echo inside the house. The crinkling of the letter in her pocket had her blowing a heavy sigh, struggling to calm down, as she listened to the bustle of footsteps on the other side of the door. *Relax.*

The locks rattled noisily, and then Jackie pulled open the door. Jayla was surprised to see that the expression on her face was more expectant than anything as her wide frame filled the doorway. "I figured you would make it this way sooner or later," Jackie said as she stepped to the side.

Jayla nodded. She entered the foyer and made her way to the living room. Jackie must have been on some "I'm Every Woman"–type empowerment trip after she put Quentin out. The home had been completely redecorated in rich purple hues, with splashes of black and silver to accent the purple. Family pictures on the mantel had been replaced with abstract art pieces, and a brand-new TV played on mute on a glass TV stand in a corner of the room. A white Christmas tree was adorned with red and green ornaments, and its string of lights illuminated a few gifts and children's toys underneath. Jayla frowned when she noticed the infant mat and teething toys scattered in the middle of the floor.

"Babysitting," Jackie said, as if reading her thoughts, and she made no move to explain any further.

Jayla nodded again as she took a seat on the plush sectional. It wasn't like it was her business anyway. Besides, they had more important things to discuss.

Jackie sat opposite her in the recliner. For a moment, neither spoke, and the awkward silence felt suffocating. "Listen," she finally said, speaking up first. She ran her nervous fingers through her hair. "Let me just say that I'm sorry for writing a letter, as opposed to telling you in person. There was really no easy way to break that to you."

The words from the letter confession were still piercing Jayla's brain, as if they had been branded. She wouldn't have believed them to be true had Jackie not admitted to handwriting the letter herself. The shit was still baffling.

"Jackie, I don't know what to say about any of it." Jayla sighed weakly. The pain was definitely eating at her. "I tried to be mad at you, but that almost made it seem like I wasn't acknowledging the foul shit I did by even fucking with him in the first place. But I thought I loved him. I wanted us to be in a relationship. He just wanted to cheat around on you before you two settled down, so he fed me all the young teenage shit I wanted to hear. But I was serious about him. He made it clear that he really loved you, though, so I figured getting pregnant would convince him to leave you and be with me instead. I didn't see anything wrong with that." As she spoke, Jayla saw her sister's jaw clench, and she knew the admission was probably pissing her off.

Jayla went on. "I'm wrong, okay? I understand that. I was selfish and reckless, and I deserved every piece of shit karma threw my way. I'm so angry and so hurt by what you did. We probably won't ever speak again after this visit, to be honest with you. But . . ." Jayla paused, nibbling on her bottom lip, as she struggled to contain the overwhelming feelings that threatened to spill out. "I'm just as angry and hurt at myself for even initiating any of this to begin with. Does that make sense?"

Jackie's nod was slow as she digested the information. "Yeah," she said. "Makes perfect sense." A flicker of appreciation shone in her eyes before it was replaced with her blank gaze. She looked as if she had something else to say.

"What is it?" Jayla prompted when Jackie kept her lips pursed together.

"Did you have anything to do with Mama's death?" Jackie asked quietly.

Jayla lowered her eyes, the unspoken answer as clear as if she had screamed it out loud. She felt her sister's stare burning a hole into her face, and she waited for Jackie to pick that weight up and come flying across the room to break her apart.

"You know, the police called me," Jackie said. "They were asking me about you and what happened that night. I didn't tell them anything."

Jayla rolled her eyes. "Yeah right," she mumbled.

"I swear I didn't," Jackie said, her lips tightening into a grim frown. "But don't think for a minute I did it for you. I did it to save my own ass. They open that case and shit could come out surrounding what happened with inducing your labor and the false adoption with Jasmine. Arrows could start pointing my way if they dig up phone records and receipts and shit. It was too sketchy. So, I told them some bogus mess to get them off our asses."

"Which was?"

"The same story you gave them the first time. My mother was a drunk and a frequent abuser of drugs and liquor," Jackie spat, wincing at her own slanderous words. "I even made up a few stories about catching her doped up myself but not telling, because I didn't want her actions to separate me and my sisters. Isn't that what you told the police when she first died? Something like that?"

Jayla swallowed the knot in her throat and glanced away from her sister's penetrating stare. She knew the police had no evidence against her. They were just spinning their wheels, trying to make something out of nothing. But Heather's interrogation was resonating in her mind. "Quentin knows," she said. "I told him. He's the one that gave them the tip."

"I know. He told me he went to the police." Jackie sucked her teeth. "Don't worry. I lit into his ass. I told him if he kept running his mouth, I was going to go to the police about how he raped you when you were fourteen."

Jayla's mouth dropped open. "He didn't, but could they still charge him?"

“Don’t know,” Jackie admitted with a nonchalant shrug. “Probably not, because it’s been some years. I really don’t know how that works with rape cases, specifically statutory rape cases. But, hell, his dumb ass doesn’t know that. And I don’t think it even matters when I tell them he knowingly infected you with HIV. That’s a felony. But even if they push the case or not, he would be slandered. Down-low brotha rapes wife’s minor sister and knowingly infects her with HIV. The media would have a fucking field day. If he’s convicted, the prisoners would eat his ass alive. If he’s not, the community damn sure would do it instead.”

Jayla almost had to chuckle to herself. They were sitting up here discussing framing Jackie’s husband, also her ex-boyfriend, for rape as nonchalantly as they would discuss catching a matinee before dinner. Jayla had forgotten how ruthless her sister could be sometimes when she felt someone had crossed her. An image of Jackie pushing her out of the moving car in the middle of the interstate played in slow motion in front of her eyes, and she shuddered at the thought. She had no words, so she said the only thing that came to mind. “Thanks, Jackie.”

Jackie shook her head. “It wasn’t for you,” she said quietly. “Trust. But since we were both in the fire, I had to snatch you out, too, or I would’ve burned with you.”

Jayla was itching to ask her if she had caught HIV, but decided against it. Sometimes ignorance was bliss. She didn't know if she could stomach knowing her sister had it too. Not now. Not with everything else going on between them.

A movement on the muted TV caught Jayla's attention, and she focused on the screen. The video footage of Grant being handcuffed and escorted into the courthouse. Again. They had been replaying the story nonstop all afternoon. Apparently, his first-degree murder charge was a hotter story than the leaked photos of his sexual exploits had been. The media hadn't bothered her since he was arrested nearly a month ago.

Jackie's eyes followed Jayla's to the TV, and she sat back in the recliner with a frustrated sigh. "I'll be glad when they charge him and get the shit over with," she said, more to herself than to her sister. "I know they proved how Jasmine killed his son, but to think they're giving him more glory now than when he was in office. The shit is twisted. I loved Jasmine, but I can admit my daughter was sick, and she needed psychological help. Not to be murdered. No, we weren't close at all anymore, but it still hurts to see everyone at this man's feet, like what he did wasn't wrong."

Jayla kept her mouth shut. She knew Jasmine's murder was still a very sore spot for her sister, and she doubted that reminding her of how Jasmine had deserved it would bring much comfort. Especially since she had arranged her death. If only Jackie knew just how deep the rabbit hole went. Jayla knew she would probably be lying next to her daughter six feet under.

Jayla could have just stuck with Sheila's original plan to frame Jasmine for Marcus's murder. Jasmine would have gone to jail, and that would have been the end of it. But when Jayla had seen how Jasmine piped up about her mental illness and they transferred her to the behavioral health center, Jayla hadn't been satisfied with that. The shit wasn't fair. After all Jasmine had done, hanging around in a mental hospital for a few years until she got out on good behavior was hardly a punishment that fit the crime. So, Jayla had gone along with the Mommy-daughter best friend role-playing, and Jasmine, like the naive little girl she was, had played right into her hands.

But more than anything, Jayla had recognized that Jasmine was headed down her same path, and as her mother, she could not have let her keep it up. Jasmine had gotten so out of control already, and there was no telling how much more destruction she would wreak. Jayla faulted herself for the monster she had created. Now she took responsibility for the monster she had destroyed. It still didn't make it any easier to sleep at night, but she was slowly pushing her past out of her mind in order to move forward. She had to.

Jackie was studying her again. Her face clearly reflected that she was suspicious of Jayla's silence, but she didn't say anything. And Jayla didn't either. That was what their relationship had come to. The best hidden secrets were the ones that went unmentioned. Consequently, tension hung thick in the air between them.

"Jackie, do you remember Grant being around when you were little? Before I was born?" Jayla finally asked, breaking the silence.

"Not really," Jackie revealed. "I was young, and Mama didn't bring her boyfriends around me. I just remember she ended up pregnant with you, but that's it." She paused when Jayla just nodded her head and closed her eyes. "So, it's true what they're saying about you and Grant?"

Jayla nodded again and looked down at the floor. "Yeah. It's true. He's my father." She didn't even bother looking up when she said those words. But she could almost feel the stunned expression on Jackie's face.

"So, now what?"

"What do you mean, now what? I can't do anything about it now." Jayla gestured toward the TV, where Grant's lawyer was talking to the cameras. "The man is on trial for murder. I slept with him. We haven't been able to have a relationship thus far, so there is nothing for us now."

The truth stung even as the words left her lips. She wished it could've been different. She kept wondering what her life would have been like had Patricia not intervened. What her life would have been like growing up with both parents.

Would she still have turned out the same? All the major events in her life—HIV, sleeping with her sister's boyfriend, her pregnancy, her mother's death, meeting Patricia, and the Heartbreaker business—would never have happened. Without Patricia's interference, there was no way she would be the person she was now. And that thought alone left a dark, aching hole in her heart.

Maybe one day she would go visit Grant. A part of her yearned to establish a real relationship with him. One not built on lies and deception. God knows, the poor man had been a pawn in too many women's vicious games.

A baby's whimpers had Jackie climbing to her feet. She left the room and, to Jayla's surprise, returned with an adorable baby boy with chubby cheeks and curious eyes, who stared at the visitor through dried tears. Jackie popped a pacifier in the boy's mouth, and he took greedy sucks on the rubber nipple. "This is Derrick," Jackie said, rubbing his leg affectionately. "We call him DJ. He is just the cutest thing." She nuzzled his neck, and DJ responded with a giddy laugh while still managing to clutch the pacifier between his gums.

Jayla let out a breath as the revelation hit her. She remembered Derrick had adopted Tara's baby. Damn, seeing DJ brought on a fresh bout of heartache. "How are they anyway?" She struggled to come off as nonchalant, but her curiosity was all too obvious.

"They're good," Jackie said. "They're happy." Her words were as much an explanation as they were a warning.

Jayla took the hint and nodded. She would heal. It hurt, but she had been through worse.

Jackie turned and headed to the kitchen. Just then the doorbell rang, and she called over her shoulder, "Can you get that please, Jayla?"

Jayla rose from the sectional, trotted to the foyer, and pulled open the front door. A young woman in crisp slacks and a chic military blazer stood on the porch. Her outfit was an odd contrast to the diaper bag that hung on one of her arms and the rolling Dora the Explorer suitcase, the handle of which she grasped with her other hand. A baby carrier rested at her feet.

"Hi," she said. "Is Jasmine's mother here?"

Jayla frowned, unsure how to answer that question. "May I ask who you are?"

"I'm Kendra. I'm a friend—or I was a friend—of Jasmine's. I know this is a bad time, but I really need to speak to her mother."

At that moment, Jackie, balancing DJ on her hip, joined Jayla at the front door, and she, too, squinted in confusion at the visitor on her porch. "Nice to finally meet you, Kendra," she greeted. "I'm sure you heard what happened to Jasmine."

Kendra glanced down and nodded, blinking back tears. "Yeah, I know. But I still needed to come by to talk to you. I'm about to catch a flight out in a few hours. I'm moving to California. But I still have Jasmine's daughter."

"Daughter?" Jayla and Jackie said in unison, both of them shocked.

"Yes. She didn't tell you?"

"I didn't even know Jasmine was pregnant," Jackie said, her eyes dropping to the carrier. "Are you sure that's her kid?"

Kendra hesitated, eyeing both women, as if she wasn't sure how to respond. "I was there," she said finally. "Unfortunately, Jasmine wasn't the best mother, and she always put Gabrielle off on me. Needless to say, I'm not trying to be a single mother, and I'm not ready to be tied down with a kid. I was wondering if you would take her."

Jayla was still riding high on the shock of the situation. Her heart went out to the baby. Poor Gabrielle hadn't asked to be here, and now she was an orphan. All because her stupid mother had sexed any piece of dick that could slide her some coins. "Where is the baby's father?" she asked.

Kendra shrugged. "I don't know. I don't even know who he is." She sighed when both women remained rooted in place, as if frozen stiff by the news. "Look, I'm sorry to drop this on you. But Jasmine was a friend, and now she's dead. I don't know what else to do. If you don't want her daughter, I can just take her to DFCS or the police department or something. Hell, I really don't know. I just know I can't keep her."

"No, it's fine," Jackie said with a small smile. "We'll take her. She has family, so no need to throw her into the system. Thank you for bringing her here."

Kendra nodded, and with a relieved sigh, she let go of the suitcase and handed over the diaper bag to Jayla before heading down the porch stairs to Jasmine's Bentley, which was waiting in the driveway.

Jayla picked up the carrier and couldn't help but grin at the gorgeous baby doll nestled in the pink fleece blanket. She was adorable, and Jayla's heart melted at the sight of her.

"Damn, that's crazy," Jackie said, switching DJ to her other hip so she could grab the suitcase. "When did Jasmine have a baby?"

"I don't know. We don't even know when her birthday is. You think she packed the birth certificate and all her records?"

"Hell, I don't know." Jackie said as they went back into the house, their hands full.

They returned to the living room, and Jackie sat DJ on his play mat, and immediately he busied himself with his toys. Jackie collapsed back on the recliner and let out a weary sigh. "What the hell am I going to do with an infant, Jayla? Do you know how old I am? Plus, I'm going through a divorce. I don't have time to be dealing with this right now. And I'm supposed to start over all of a sudden by raising my grandchild?"

Jayla sat on the sectional with the carrier on her lap. The baby was sleeping so deeply, she didn't want to disturb her by taking her out of the seat. She wasn't really sure how to feel either. But she knew pity was tearing at her as she gazed lovingly down at the innocent face.

Jackie watched Jayla as she stared at the baby, and a sudden idea had the weight of this new responsibility lifting from her shoulders. "Why don't you take her, Jayla?"

Jayla's head whipped up from surprise. "What?"

"You're in a better position to take care of her than me."

Jayla's mouth hung open as she tried to contain the spark of excitement quickening her heart. She didn't know anything about raising a baby. And given her life—well, the life she was leaving behind—she didn't want to risk messing up poor Gabrielle's like she had Jasmine's. She was still trying to heal from that fuckup.

"Jayla, you're Jasmine's mother too," Jackie went on, with an encouraging nod. "I raised her, but you would have if I had given you the opportunity. Here is your opportunity. We're even now."

As if on cue, the baby stirred and began to whine. Jayla slipped her finger in Gabrielle's tiny hand,

and she gripped it hard. It must have comforted her enough, because she soon was snoring lightly. Jayla gazed at the little fist that gripped her finger, and her heart swelled. Was this her second chance? Her phone rang at that moment, and she used her free hand to fish it out of her pocket.

The name on the caller ID had her grin spreading, and she took the call. "Hey, sweetie," she answered.

"Hey, you," Kelton greeted.

She could almost hear the smile in his voice as he spoke. She and Kelton had been taking it extremely slow but steady over the past few weeks. She still didn't trust herself or the relationship, but she was willing to see where it led by treading lightly.

"I'm letting you know I'm off. Why don't you meet me and my son at the park? Then maybe we can go grab some dinner."

"Sounds like a plan." Jayla looked at Gabrielle with renewed love, which almost brought tears to her eyes. She remembered Kelton telling her during their first dinner together that his newborn baby girl had died in the hospital shortly after her birth. Maybe, just maybe, this was karma finally throwing her a lifeline. They hung up.

She had been tempted to tell him about her past. About her destructive Heartbreaker business. But she was guarding her heart with everything in her.

Her past indiscretions were on a need-to-know basis, and she would take it slow, telling him if she needed to. If he didn't accept it, so be it. She had already revealed her HIV positive status, and he was surprisingly understanding. But even if the little thing between them fizzled and died out, she would be okay. Hell, she had been through worse, and she was stronger now. Much stronger. And now even more so, because she needed to be strong for Gabrielle. Her daughter. She couldn't be sure if she had two years left or twenty, but she would make sure to take advantage of each day she lived to see another.

Her web of deceit had had her so tangled up, she had nearly strangled herself. From this point forward, there would be no more secrets. Well, no more *new* secrets. The ones she had would just stay buried. If they didn't, well, Kelton was a cop, and he could be persuaded to take care of some things for her. She had figured as much when she first set out to hook him at the police station.

And, like all men, he had taken the bait.

The End